'**Do I make you nervous?**' Leo asked from behind her. She could hear the laughter in his voice. Deliberately she turned, dropping her hand away from her neck. *Calm, cool.*

'Of course not,' Anna said.

He winked. 'Good. Because I'm afraid the jeans are next, darling. I can't abide wet clothing.'

Anna held her breath as his long fingers flicked open the button of his jeans. She couldn't have looked away if her life depended on it. Her heart kicked up as his hip bones appeared, but she forgot all about it as the jeans slid down his long, strong legs, revealing tanned skin and acres of muscle. Anna couldn't breathe.

Could this day be any more surreal? Just a few minutes ago, they'd been fully clothed strangers. And now they were marooned together and Leo was stripping out of his clothing.

'Keep staring, darling, and the show is bound to get more interesting,' Leo said, his voice a growling purr that slid over her nerve endings and made her shudder.

'I've seen naked men before,' she said with a sniff. 'You can't shock me.'

It was only a small lie.

SANTINA CROWN

Royalty has never been so scandalous!

STOP PRESS—Crown Prince in shock marriage

The tabloid headlines…

When HRH Crown Prince Alessandro of Santina proposes to paparazzi favourite Allegra Jackson it promises to be the social event of the decade —outrageous headlines guaranteed!

The salacious gossip…

Mills & Boon invites you to rub shoulders with royalty, sheikhs and glamorous socialites. Step into the decadent playground of the world's rich and famous…

THE SANTINA CROWN

THE SANTINA CROWN

THE GIRL NOBODY WANTED

LYNN RAYE HARRIS

First published in Great Britain 2012
by Mills & Boon, an imprint of Harlequin (UK) Limited,
Eton House, 18-24 Paradise Road, Richmond, Surrey TW9 1SR

THE GIRL NOBODY WANTED © Harlequin Books S.A. 2012

Special thanks and acknowledgement are given to Lynn Raye Harris for her contribution to The Santina Crown series.

ISBN: 978 0 263 89766 1

53-0812

Harlequin (UK) policy is to use papers that are natural, renewable and recyclable products and made from wood grown in sustainable forests. The logging and manufacturing processes conform to the legal environmental regulations of the country of origin.

Printed and bound in Spain
by Blackprint CPI, Barcelona

Lynn Raye Harris read her first Mills & Boon® romance when her grandmother carted home a box from a yard sale. She didn't know she wanted to be a writer then, but she definitely knew she wanted to marry a sheikh or a prince and live the glamorous life she read about in the pages. Instead, she married a military man and moved around the world. These days she makes her home in North Alabama, with her handsome husband and two crazy cats. Writing for Mills & Boon is a dream come true. You can visit her at www.lynnrayeharris.com.

For my in-laws, Larry and Joyce Harris. Fifty years together is quite an accomplishment. You are proof that love can last forever. I'm so happy you're a part of my life, and I love you both.

CHAPTER ONE

ANNA CONSTANTINIDES stood at the edge of the gathered crowd and hoped the serene countenance she'd practiced before the mirror for the past week was holding up. Tonight was, without doubt, the most humiliating night of her life. Her fiancé—correction, former fiancé—was marrying another woman.

It would not have been so bad, perhaps, if her fiancé wasn't Prince Alessandro, heir to the Santina throne. She should have been his queen, yet she was currently the jilted bride.

A fact the media took great delight in reporting.

Again and again and *again.* She'd hardly had a peaceful moment since Alex had dumped her so publicly and humiliatingly for another woman. He hadn't even had the courtesy to inform her personally. No, he'd let her find out in the pages of the tabloids. Simply *mortifying.*

The pity she'd had to endure. The knowing

looks—even, surprisingly, a hint of censure. As if it were *her* fault somehow. As if she were the one who'd been caught kissing another man while engaged to someone else, as Alex had been photographed with Allegra Jackson.

Anna wanted nothing less than to be at his engagement party tonight, but she'd had no choice. "Anna," her mother had said when she'd refused, "you must. Protocol demands it."

"I don't give a damn about protocol," she'd replied. And she hadn't. Why, when she'd dedicated her life to protocol and duty and been so spectacularly punished for it?

Her mother took her hands. "Sweetheart, do it for me. Queen Zoe is my oldest and dearest friend. I know she would be disappointed if we were not there to support her."

Support *her?* Anna had wanted to laugh, to shout, to rail against the unfairness of life—but she had not. Ultimately, she had done precisely what her mother asked because, for pity's sake, she felt *guilty.*

Anna stiffened her spine as the king began to toast the happy couple. But she lifted her glass of champagne along with everyone else, and prepared to drink to the health and happiness of Alex and Allegra, the woman who'd turned her preordained life upside down.

At least, thank goodness, she could be certain

there were no photographers present tonight. They would be waiting outside the palace gates, naturally, but for now she was safe.

And yet she still had to smile, had to pretend she wasn't dying from embarrassment. She would have to endure the stories, the photos, the quotes from anonymous "friends" who claimed she was holding up well, or that she was fragile, or that her heart had shattered into a million pieces.

Anna sipped her champagne on cue. Only an hour more, and she was out of here. Back to the hotel where she would crawl into her bed and pull the covers over her head. The toast ended, and then the ensemble began to play a waltz. Anna slipped her barely touched glass onto a passing waiter's tray and turned toward the doors to the terrace. If she could escape for just a few moments, she could endure the next hour with a great deal more fortitude.

"Anna," a woman called. "I've been looking for you."

Anna gritted her teeth and turned toward Graziana Ricci, the Amanti foreign minister's wife. The woman sashayed toward her, a bright smile pasted on her cosmetically enhanced face. But it wasn't Signora Ricci who captured Anna's attention. It was the man beside her.

An Englishman, she assumed, as there were so many who had descended upon Santina recently.

He was tall, dressed in a bespoke tuxedo like nearly every other man in the room, and quite striking. Handsome, in a boyish way that somehow wasn't boyish at all. No, it was devilish, as if he knew the temptation he offered merely by existing. Eyes the color of roast coffee glittered in a face that had been carved by Michelangelo. Somehow, the look in those eyes dared her to envision him naked atop a pedestal.

Anna shook herself. Perhaps he was a work of art, but he had not been carved by Michelangelo. How silly.

But he could have been. His face was a study in angles sculpted for the sole purpose of making the owner appear sinfully irresistible to the female of the species. Sharply defined cheeks, a blade-straight nose, firm sensual lips and a small cleft at the base of his chin that deepened when he smiled.

And when he turned that smile on her, her heart skipped a beat.

Several beats.

The picture that filled her mind at that moment was decidedly uncharacteristic of her. She had absolutely no desire to kiss this man, no matter what her mind conjured up. It was stress, pure and simple.

As were the skipped beats. *Stress.*

The man smiled and winked, and Anna very

deliberately looked away. *Honestly, what was wrong with her?*

"Anna, this is Leo Jackson," Signora Ricci said, and Anna instantly stiffened. The other woman didn't notice as she giggled, hugging his arm to her surgically enhanced body. *Shameless hussy.* "Leo is Allegra's brother."

As if he could be anyone else.

"How nice," Anna said frostily, her heart careening out of control with anger and helpless frustration. Allegra's brother. As if his sister ruining her life weren't enough, she now had to be faced with another Jackson when she quite simply wished them all to hell. Which wasn't very polite or charitable of her, she knew, but it was how she felt right now. "Welcome to Santina, Mr. Jackson. If you will excuse me, I was just on my way to…to an appointment."

It was a lie and her face flamed the instant she said it. Not because she cared that she'd lied, but because Leo Jackson arched one perfect eyebrow as if he knew she wanted to escape him. His lips quirked, and the flame inside her burned hotter.

But was it embarrassment or something else?

Embarrassment, she decided firmly. There could certainly be no other reason for it. If not for his sister, she wouldn't be in this predicament now. She wouldn't be standing here enduring the humiliation of hundreds of eyes surreptitiously turning upon her every time Alex leaned in close to his new fiancée and whispered something in her ear.

"I'm sorry to hear that, Anna," Leo said, using her given name as if he had every right in the world. Arrogant man! But her skin prickled with heat at the way her name sounded when he said it. Soft, sexy, alluring. Not boring Anna, but beautiful, exciting Anna.

"Nevertheless," she said, standing as straight and tall as she could. "It is the case."

What was wrong with her? Why was she being fanciful? She was simply Anna. And that's precisely who she wanted to be. Anna was safe, predictable, quietly elegant. She was not bold or brassy. Nothing like Signora Ricci, thank heavens.

Signora Ricci's mouth turned down in an exaggerated frown. "This will not take but a moment. I had hoped you could show Leo around Amanti tomorrow. He is thinking of building a luxury hotel."

Anna glanced at Leo Jackson. There was something dark and intense behind those eyes, no matter that one corner of his mouth turned up in a mocking grin. A fire began to burn low in her belly. She might be the tourist ambassador to the neighboring island of Amanti, but that didn't mean she had to personally show this man the sights.

It wasn't safe. *He* wasn't safe. She felt it in her bones.

Besides, his sister had stolen her future, and even if that wasn't his fault, she couldn't forget it if she were forced to spend time with him. No, she wanted nothing to do with this man—with *anyone* named Jackson.

"I'm afraid that's not possible, Signora Ricci. I have other things to attend to. I can arrange for someone else—"

The other woman scoffed. "What is more important than Amanti's economy? This would be good for us, yes? And you are the best for the job. What else do you have to do now that you have no wedding to prepare for?"

Anna swallowed her tongue as bitter acid scoured her throat. If she weren't a dignified person, a calm and controlled person, she might just strangle Graziana Ricci where she stood.

But no, Anna Constantinides had more dignity than that. She'd been raised to be serene, to be a perfect queen. She would not break because one woman dared to insult her on a day when she'd already been insulted by her ex-fiancé and the overwhelming media coverage of his new engagement. She was strong. She could handle this.

"If tomorrow doesn't work," Leo interjected,

"the next day surely will." He pulled a card from his pocket and held it out. "My personal number. Call me when you are available."

Anna accepted the card because to do otherwise would be rude. His fingers brushed hers, and a tongue of fire sizzled along her nerve endings. She snatched her hand back, certain she'd find her skin blackened where he'd touched her. Graziana Ricci had turned away, distracted by an elderly matron who gesticulated wildly about something.

"I'm not sure when that will be, Mr. Jackson. It might truly be better for someone else to take you."

"And yet you are the tourist ambassador," he said with a hint of steel underlying the polite veneer in his tone. "Unless, of course, you do not like me for some reason?"

Anna swallowed. "I don't know you. How could I possibly dislike you?"

His gaze cut toward the front of the room where Alex and Allegra were currently standing close together and talking in hushed tones. "How indeed?"

Anna thrust her chin out. It was bad enough she had to endure this night, but for this man to know how she felt? It was insupportable. "Tell me about this hotel you propose to build," she said. "How will this help Amanti?"

His gaze slid down her body, heat trailing behind it. *Dangerous,* a voice whispered.

He took his time meeting her eyes again. "Have you not heard of the Leonidas Group?"

She was proud of herself for not showing her surprise. If the Leonidas Group wanted to build a hotel on Amanti, that could be a very good thing. "Of course I have. They own some of the most luxurious hotels in the world and cater to the wealthiest of clients. Do you work for them, Mr. Jackson?"

His laughter was rich, rolling from him in golden tones that vibrated through her. "I own the Leonidas Group, Anna."

Again with her name, and again with the prickle of awareness skimming along her nerve endings. "How fortunate for Amanti," she said, because she could think of nothing else to say. She felt like a fool for missing the *Leo* in *Leonidas,* though it wasn't an immediately obvious connection. But if he owned the Leonidas Group, he must be very wealthy indeed.

He leaned in closer. "Perhaps you will change your mind about tomorrow, then."

Heat coiled tightly inside her. His voice was a delicious rumble in her ear, though she tried not to notice precisely how delicious. She was tired, that was all. He was just a man, and men were fickle. Unpredictable. Dishonorable.

She closed her eyes, her heart thrumming steadily. It was uncharitable to think of Alex that way, and yet she couldn't help it. He'd made a promise, damn him!

"I will have to check my calendar," she said coolly.

His smile made her heart skip a beat. Too, too charming. Perhaps his sister was equally as charming. Perhaps that's how she'd stolen Alex away.

"And yet, when you wake up and see the morning papers, you will no doubt wish yourself far from Santina."

A current of dread slid through her, icy fingers scraping her soul. The papers. They would be filled with news of Alex and Allegra tomorrow—and she would be mentioned side by side with them. The poor jilted bride. The faithful girl who'd been stood up by a prince. Sad little heiress, no longer a queen-in-waiting.

Anna's throat constricted. She absolutely did not want to be here tomorrow. And he was giving her a way out, though she would have to endure his company. But which was worse? The media frenzy, or Leo Jackson?

If she took him to Amanti, they wouldn't escape the attention entirely, but at least they would be out of Alex and Allegra's proximity. Perhaps the press might not think her so sad and distraught if she were seen going about her duties.

"I've just remembered," she said, proud that she managed to sound so cold and detached. Professional. "My appointment isn't for tomorrow after all. I keep getting my days mixed up. It's for the next day."

"Is that so?" Leo said, his gaze slipping over her once more. There was heat and promise in that voice, and a hint of possession, as well. It infuriated her—and intrigued her.

"If you wish to tour Amanti," she said crisply, already partially regretting the impulse that had her choosing him over tomorrow's papers, "we can leave around nine in the morning."

"Nine?" he mocked. "I doubt I'll have slept off tonight's debaucheries by then."

Anna felt her ears going hot. She refused to picture *any* debauchery. "Nine o'clock, Mr. Jackson. Or not at all."

"You drive a hard bargain, darling," he drawled, as if he weren't in the least bit dangerous to her sense of well-being. "But we'll do it your way."

Before she knew what he was about, he caught her hand and pressed a kiss to the back of it. Her skin tingled as his warm breath washed over her, his beautiful lips skimming so lightly over her flesh. She couldn't suppress the small shudder that racked her body or the ache of sensation that made her crave more of his touch.

Leo Jackson looked up, his gaze sharp. Too sharp. As if he'd seen through to the core of her and knew what she'd been thinking. That devilish grin was back as his coffee-colored eyes glittered with heat. "Tomorrow, darling," he said. "I look forward to it."

Anna pulled her hand away, tried very hard to ignore the pulsing throb in her belly, between her legs. "I'm not your darling, Mr. Jackson."

He winked. "Not yet. But let's see what tomorrow brings, shall we?"

After a restless night, Anna rose early the next morning, and then showered and dressed with care. She was the tourist ambassador to Amanti, not a woman going on a date, so she chose a fashionable skirt and blazer. She paired the gray suit with a red silk camisole—her one nod to color—her pearls, and gray suede pumps. She wrapped her long dark hair in a neat knot and secured it with pins. Then she slipped on mascara and lip gloss before walking over to the cheval glass and studying her reflection from head to toe.

She looked professional, competent. Precisely the way she wanted to appear. She absolutely did not care whether Leo Jackson found her attractive or not.

Liar.

Anna frowned at herself. She wasn't unattractive; she was professional. And she intended to stay that way. If she could control nothing else about these chaotic past few weeks, she could at least control her image. And this was the image she wanted to project. Serenity in the face of turmoil. Grace under fire. A calm port in the storm.

Anna patted her hair one last time before she whirled away from the mirror, found her handbag and cell phone, checked her calendar to make sure she'd taken care of everything and left her room at precisely twenty to nine. Her room was two floors up from Leo Jackson's room, but first she took an elevator down to the dining room and grabbed a quick cup of coffee and a whole-grain muffin before going back up to Leo's floor. At three minutes to nine, she knocked on his door.

Nothing happened. Anna frowned as she listened for movement behind the door. She checked her watch, studied the sweep of the second hand across the mother-of-pearl face. At nine o'clock precisely, she knocked again. "Mr. Jackson?" she said, pressing her face close to the door in order not to wake any of the other late-sleeping guests in nearby rooms. "Are you in there?"

Two minutes later, when she'd knocked yet again—louder this time, because she was getting very annoyed—the door jerked open.

Anna's stomach flipped at the sight of Leo Jackson in all his bad-boy glory. Heavens above, why did this man have to be so compelling? She should feel nothing for him but contempt. Not only had his family wrecked her perfect life, but he was also not the sort of man a proper lady should ever get involved with.

Yet heat bloomed in her cheeks as she thought of his comment last night about debauchery. Because that's precisely what he looked like— as if he'd spent the night in some lucky woman's bed, debauching her thoroughly.

Before she could control herself, Anna thought that *she* wanted to be debauched. Thoroughly. Repeatedly.

If she could have slapped her palms to her cheeks in horror, she would have done so. She most definitely did *not* want to be debauched— and certainly not by this rogue.

"Hello, darling," Leo said casually, his sensual lips twisting in that arrogant grin that had featured so prominently in her thoughts last night while she'd tossed and turned in her bed. And yet, in the moment before he'd spoken, she'd sensed something behind that playboy demeanor, something tightly leashed in and controlled.

A sleek, dangerous beast on a tether.

"Mr. Jackson," she replied coolly, hoping he

couldn't see the thrum of her pulse in her throat. "We had an appointment at nine, I believe."

He ran a hand through his dark hair. His eyes gleamed with interest as his gaze slipped over her. He had a day's growth of beard on his face—and she'd never seen anything sexier in her life.

Neither, it seemed, had some other woman. Or, heaven forbid, *women*. Yes, she definitely could see Leo Jackson taking more than one woman home with him at a time.

Oh, dear... The images in her head were definitely not safe for public consumption.

But he stood in the door, looking so dissolute and sexy in his tuxedo from last night she couldn't form a coherent thought as she studied him. The beast was concealed once more, so that she found herself wondering if she'd imagined it. But she had not, she was certain. He was smooth and magnificent—and not quite what he seemed to be at first glance.

His jacket hung open and his shirt was unbuttoned. The tie and studs were gone, probably tucked into a pocket. A bright smudge of pink was smeared across the pristine white of his collar. Lipstick, she realized with a jolt. And not the color Graziana Ricci had been wearing.

She was positive, looking at him, that he'd not spent the night in his own bed. In fact, she was pretty sure he hadn't slept at all. She tried not to think of what he'd been doing instead—or whom he'd been doing it with.

While she had lain awake thinking about this man, he'd forgotten all about her. Clearly, as his lack of readiness and his delay in answering the door indicated. She only hoped her cheeks weren't scarlet. What if he had a woman in there right now?

"I—I can come back later," she blurted. "If you're, um, busy."

"Not at all," he said smoothly, wrapping a hand around her elbow and pulling her into the room. She caught her heel and stumbled to a halt in the small foyer of his suite, her hands automatically bracing against his chest as she nearly lost her balance.

"Sorry about that, darling," he said, his arms enveloping her. His broad hands were on her back, her waist, searing into her like a flaming-hot brand. Her heart skittered. She had an impression of a sleeping lion rearing its head and sniffing the air for prey.

"I don't think you're sorry at all," she bit out, and then stifled a gasp when she realized what she'd said. No matter how she felt about Leo Jackson, it wasn't permissible to be rude. She'd spent a lifetime learning the art of diplomacy, a skill she would have needed as Queen of

Santina one day. And she'd just failed miserably, hadn't she?

No wonder Alex had left her. Except, how was Allegra Jackson any better suited to be a queen, considering how scandalously her family had behaved last night?

If appearances were any indication, *this* particular Jackson had behaved very badly indeed.

Leo laughed, the fingers of one hand caressing the furrow of her spine through her clothing. Oh, if he kept doing that… Heat and light flared inside her, slid through her limbs until she wanted to mold herself to him like a second skin. His body was hard against hers, hot. It disconcerted her, and thrilled her. How could she react to this man so soon after Alex had turned her world upside down?

"Since you've landed in my arms, perhaps I'm not sorry," he said.

No man had ever held her so close. Not even Alex. She'd learned to dance with men, to conduct herself with poise and grace, and she'd been in a man's embrace before. But not this kind of embrace. This hot, needy, sensual embrace that was, on the surface, not improper at all.

Except for how it made her feel. Oh, yes, she felt quite improper when Leo Jackson had his arms around her. As if she wanted to feel skin against skin, mouth against mouth. As if she wanted to burn up in his arms and see what it felt like.

Ridiculous, since she didn't even know him. The stress of the past few weeks had obviously affected her brain.

Anna disentangled herself from his embrace and took a step back. She tugged on the bottom of her jacket to straighten it. Then she patted her hair, happy that no stray wisps had escaped the confinement of her knot.

Leo shook his head as he studied her with an expression of bemusement on his face. "Afraid of what you might feel if you let yourself go, darling?"

Fire burst through her, making twin spots rise in her cheeks. "Stop calling me *darling*," she said firmly. "And stop trying to seduce me, Mr. Jackson. It won't work."

She wouldn't *let* it work.

The gleam in his eyes was predatory. Feral. Exciting.

Dangerous.

"Really? Not feeling the least bit angry about your fiancé and my sister? Not aching to put it all behind you with a few pleasurable hours?"

Anna lifted her chin. He'd seen right through her, hadn't he? "Actually, that sounds quite lovely. But first I'll need to find someone to spend those hours with."

"I'm wounded," he said lightly, though something in his expression made her take a step back.

"I doubt that," she replied crisply. "You'll have moved on to the next woman on your list without a moment's regret, I'm certain. We are all interchangeable to you."

Was that irritation flaring in his dark eyes? Anger?

Or pain? It shocked her enough that she couldn't decide. But then it was gone so quickly she began to wonder if she'd imagined it. Did she want him to have a conscience so it would make this strange attraction to him more bearable?

Probably.

Still, her outburst went against everything she'd ever been taught. She was out of her depth lately, stressed and furious and hurt. She had to govern herself better. "Forget I said that. It was rude."

"And you can't stand being rude, can you, Anna?" His voice caressed her name exactly as she'd imagined it last night, while lying awake in her bed.

"It's not the way I was raised," she said primly. Then she glanced at her watch, because the air felt suddenly thick and hot and she didn't know what else to do. "We're running late, Mr. Jackson. Our boat is at the dock. We were supposed to leave five minutes ago."

"Heaven forbid we are late. But you can cancel

the boat. The tour will go much faster if we take my plane."

Anna blinked. "Plane? Amanti is only twenty-five miles away by sea. The boat will have us there in under an hour, and then we can hire a car to take us around the island."

His expression was patient but firm. "I need to see the coast. We'll fly around the island first, and then land and have a tour, yes?"

Anna reached for her pearls, comforting herself with the solid feel of them between her fingers. He was overriding all her plans. It was too much like what had happened to her life lately, and it made her nervous. Uncertain. Damn, how she hated that feeling.

"But I've already arranged things," she said firmly, attempting to regain control of the situation. "There is no need for you to put yourself out, Mr. Jackson."

He reached for her again, put his hands on either side of her shoulders and bent until his gorgeous eyes were on a level with hers. Her heart flipped. "Arrangements can be changed, Anna. And you really need to call me Leo."

She darted her tongue over her lower lip. "I'd prefer to keep this professional, if you don't mind."

"I do mind," he said, his eyes darkening.

Anna tried not to let the warm, spicy scent of

him wrap around her senses. But he was too close, and he smelled so good, and her stomach was knotting with tension at his proximity. He confused her. She ached in ways she never had before, and she wanted things she'd once looked upon with quiet acceptance. She'd expected to be intimate with Alex, of course. She hadn't expected to find out she wanted that intimacy with a kind of earthy sensuality that was completely foreign to her nature.

But not with Alex.

With this man. With Leo.

"Keep looking at me that way, and we won't go anywhere," he murmured, his voice a lovely growl in his throat. She imagined him growling against her skin, his body twining intimately with hers, and swallowed hard.

It was shocking to be thinking these thoughts. And so very, *very* titillating.

She might be a virgin, but she wasn't stupid. She was modern enough to have read a few books on sex. She'd even managed to watch a video, the memory of which had her heart hurtling forward. The way the man had put his head between the woman's legs and—

"Anna," Leo groaned. "Stop."

Anna shook herself. What was wrong with her? Baiting a lion in his den? Was she insane?

"Really, I have no idea what you're talking about Mr.—Leo. You have a very dirty mind."

His sharp bark of laughter was not quite what she expected. He let her go abruptly, and her skin tingled through her clothes where he'd so recently touched her. "I think if this tour stands a chance of getting off the ground, I'd better change."

"That would be wise," she said primly.

She stood in the foyer, uncertain whether to follow or stay where she was. In the end, she decided to stay. She could hear him moving around, hear a soft curse as a door opened and shut again. She looked at her reflection in the mirror, blushed anew at her heightened color. Leo Jackson brought out the worst in her.

She was just beginning to worry about how long she'd been standing there when he reappeared. A jolt of surprise went through her at the sight of him. She didn't know what she'd expected, but his casual attire had not quite been it.

He wore a long-sleeved navy shirt, unbuttoned midchest, with a white T-shirt beneath. Half the shirt was tucked into faded, ripped jeans. The other half hung free in a kind of casual slouch that proclaimed this man didn't care about rules.

But the truth was that he looked utterly gorgeous. The height of Bohemian fashion, while she stood there in her prim suit and felt frumpy. Stuffy. Oh, the suit was expensive, but it was staid. Safe and boring. A generation too old for her, perhaps. The stylist had tried to get her to go with a shorter hem, a nipped-in waist, but she'd refused.

She was regretting it at the moment.

"Ready, my love?" he asked, and her heart skipped a beat.

"Only if you stop calling me names," she said, her jaw aching with the effort it took to be polite as she forced the words out.

He grinned, and her heart melted. Damn it. Damn *him*.

"I can try, sweet Anna."

Somehow, that was even worse.

CHAPTER TWO

IT WAS a glorious morning in Santina. The sun was shining brightly in the sky and the turquoise water of the Mediterranean sparkled like diamonds beneath it. Anna buckled her seat belt and tried to calm the racing of her heart as their plane began to taxi toward the runway.

Leo was flying. She hadn't quite expected that. When he'd said they would take his plane, she'd assumed he had a flight crew. Which he did, but he'd given them the day off to see the sights.

"Don't you need help?" she'd asked.

"It's a small plane," he'd replied. "Certified for one pilot. I left the 737 at home this time."

"It seems like a lot of trouble to go to for a short trip."

He smiled at her, and her heart turned over. "Relax, Anna. They wouldn't let me take off if I wasn't licensed."

She had to admit that he'd done a thorough check of the plane before they'd gone anywhere.

He'd spent time looking at the instruments, walking around the craft, going over a checklist. Finally, when he'd deemed everything to be okay, he'd communicated with the tower.

And now they were turning onto the runway, the plane braking only momentarily while Leo said something else to the tower. Someone gave him the go-ahead, and then the plane was shooting down the runway. Anna bit her lip to stifle the laughter that wanted to break free at that very moment.

She loved everything about taking off. The charge down the runway, the plane lifting into the air, the ground falling away and her stomach going with it. She loved the way they soared into the sky with the landscape below getting smaller and smaller. She could see the rocky outcrop on which the palace was built, the faded terra-cotta roofs of the city, the glint of sunlight on glass and metal.

She slumped into her seat, a strange sense of relief pouring over her. She was leaving it all behind. She was free, at least for the next few hours, and her heart felt suddenly light.

She turned to look out Leo's side and caught him glancing at her. Her stomach flipped.

"Happy?" he asked, and she wondered how he knew. She hadn't given it away. She hadn't laughed, or smiled, or reacted at all. She knew because she'd practiced it for so many years. It was essential, as a queen, to be tranquil. To hide your feelings behind a mask of cool efficiency. She was good at it.

Usually.

"I don't, um, feel happy or sad," she said, stumbling in the middle and hoping he hadn't noticed.

"Liar," he shot at her. But he grinned when he said it, and a current of warmth washed over her. "I've an idea, sweet Anna."

She pointedly ignored his use of her name and the epithet he'd attached to it. "What is this idea?"

The hot, intense look he gave her had the power to melt her insides. He looked at her like he owned her, and it made little sparks fly around inside her like a racquetball bouncing off the walls of the court.

"Let's fly to Sicily. We can spend the day there, eating pasta, viewing the volcano—" one eyebrow arched, his voice dropping an octave before he said the next two words "—making love. We'll return to Amanti tonight and tour tomorrow."

Anna felt her face go red even as her heart rate notched up. "Impossible," she said.

"And why is that? Because you don't like me? You don't need to like me, Anna, for what I have in mind."

She needed a fan turned on her body full blast. "I have no feelings about you at all, Mr. Jackson."

"Really? I find that difficult to believe."

"I don't see why you should."

"Because I am a Jackson, perhaps?"

She crossed her arms and gazed out the window. Below, the ocean rolled in all directions. "I could hardly hold you responsible for what your sister has done."

He seemed to hesitate for a moment. "Whatever she has done," he said softly, "she has not done it alone."

Anna's heart burned. "No, you are quite correct. It takes two, as the saying goes."

"Indeed. Just imagine what the two of us could do together in Sicily." His voice was seductive, full of promise.

"We're going to Amanti. Now," she said firmly.

"Are you sure? I'm quite worth the side trip, I assure you."

"Good heavens, you are vain," she said, her heart racing at the thought of doing something so insane, so out of the ordinary. "No. No, no, *no*."

But a part of her wanted to say yes. She wanted to be the woman she'd never been allowed to be. She wanted to break free of her suits and her pearls and spend one glorious, hot, naked day with a man. She wanted to know what it felt like to let a man like Leo have his wicked way with her.

No, she told herself quite firmly, *she did not.*

But why not? Everything she'd prepared for, everything she'd thought her life was going to be, had disappeared in the blink of an eye. She was a virgin who'd never even kissed a man because she'd been saving herself for Alex Santina. Alex, who'd never kissed her properly. He'd brushed his lips across her cheek, once over her mouth, but the contact had been so light and perfunctory that she had no idea what it truly felt like to kiss a man.

And Leo wanted to take her to Sicily and make love to her. She shivered with excitement. It was preposterous, and she wasn't going to say yes, but the idea was rather thrilling in an illicit way that had her sex tightening in response.

A static voice came over the headset then, and she jumped in surprise at the sudden sound slicing across her thoughts. She couldn't hear what the voice said, but Leo replied. And then he was pulling on the controls and they were climbing higher and faster.

"What?" she said, her heart thudding for a different reason now. "What is it?"

"Nothing," he replied. "Some unexpected turbulence. We're climbing to avoid it."

"Why did you ask me to go to Sicily? You've filed a flight plan. You can't just change it."

Leo flashed her another of those smiles that did things to her insides. "We aren't a commercial aircraft, darling. I can change it if I wish. Haven't you heard I'm eccentric that way?"

"I've heard nothing at all about you," she said with a sniff. It was only partially true. Last night, when she'd gotten back to her room, she'd done an internet search on Leo Jackson.

"Excellent. So you won't have made up your mind about me yet."

"Oh, I'm sure I have."

"Have you now? And what have you decided?"

Anna studied his profile. Leo Jackson was handsome and wealthy, and reputed to be intense in both his business dealings and personal relationships. He was also a serial womanizer who'd spent the past several years living in the United States, dating Hollywood starlets and supermodels and, on one memorable occasion, a gorgeous actress who was at least twenty years his senior. Of all the women he'd been linked with, that was the only one that had ever seemed to be somewhat serious.

There was no indication about what had ended the relationship, but it was definitely over. The actress had recently married someone else and adopted a baby with him.

"I think you can't be trusted," she said softly.

"Ah. What a shame."

"But you don't deny it."

He shook his head. "That depends on how you

define *trust*. Will I seduce you in spite of your denials that you're attracted to me? Possibly. Will I lie to you and leave you heartbroken? Never. Because I will tell you up front that it's not wise to have expectations beyond the physical. We can have a good time, but we aren't getting married."

Anna crossed her legs. Had she really thought going to Sicily with him might be thrilling? "Why would you assume that a woman might have expectations about you? Are you truly that fabulous that no one can resist you? Honestly, I've never met anyone so arrogant as you. Not everyone thinks you're irresistible, you know."

"But you do."

Surely her face was bright red. From anger, not embarrassment, she told herself. "I do not. I don't even like you."

He laughed as if she'd admitted something she shouldn't have. "And here I thought you didn't have any feelings at all about me."

"I'm rapidly changing my mind."

The look he gave her jolted her to her core. Dark, sensual, breathtakingly intense. "We could have fun in Sicily, Anna. Hot, decadent, pleasurable fun."

Her heart was thrumming. "Please stop saying *we*. *We* aren't doing anything together, Mr. Jackson."

He laughed again. "Back to that? Have you ever

considered, sweet Anna, that perhaps it's time you let your hair down a bit? Time to let go of that buttoned-up perfection you try so hard to project and have some fun?"

Anna clenched her hands into fists in her lap. He didn't know her, didn't know what he was saying. He was simply guessing, because that's what men like him did. They got beneath your skin and made you desire them, made you think they understood you when in fact they only understood how to lower your defenses. It was a parlor trick, the kind of thing bogus fortune tellers did every day at the carnival.

She might not be experienced, but she wasn't stupid.

"You're grabbing at straws," she said calmly. "I am well aware I'm not perfect. And I like the way I'm dressed."

"It's not a bad way to dress if you're chairing a board meeting," he said. "But it's not your true style."

"I don't think you have the first clue about my style."

"I'm not sure you do, either," he said. "But we could start with naked and go from there."

Heat flared in her core, impossible heat. Her limbs were jelly whenever he mentioned the word *naked*. She was in danger of turning into a slack-jawed nitwit if he kept it up. "Do you ever quit?"

"I do," he said. "But I don't think we've reached that point yet."

Anna groaned. It was uncharacteristic of her, but she couldn't help it. "Why are you torturing me? Why can't we just fly to Amanti, view the coast and go back to Santina?"

Leo looked at her, his expression suddenly very serious. "Do you really want to go back to Santina? Is that where you want to be today?"

She turned to look out the window. The sea spread in all directions, as far as the eye could see. It was hard to believe they could be in the Mediterranean and it could still feel so remote. As if they were the only two people in the world. There were no boats out here, no other planes, nothing but the blue sky, the bright sun and dazzling water.

She was alone with him, and while he frustrated her, he also made her feel things she'd not felt before: attractive, alive, interesting. She wasn't quite ready to give that up yet.

"No," she said softly. And then she turned to face him, her jaw hardening. "No, I don't want to go back."

Leo wasn't sure why, but he wanted her. She was quite possibly the most uptight woman he'd ever met, but for some reason that intrigued him. Like now, when she sat there beside him and tried to look stony. He wasn't sure she realized it, but stony didn't really work when you had wide jade-green eyes that showed every ounce of hurt you were feeling, whether you wanted them to or not.

And Anna was hurting. He'd seen her across the room last night, looking so isolated and alone, and he'd wanted to know who she was. Graziana Ricci had laughed dismissively. "Oh, that's Anna Constantinides. The jilted bride."

The jilted bride. He'd watched her closely then, wondering what she must be feeling as she listened to the toasts to Prince Alessandro and Allegra. She'd looked so cool, so bored, so perfect and untouchable dressed all in icy white—but then her fingers had strayed to the pearl necklace she wore, and he'd noticed they were trembling. When she'd turned toward him, the light from the chandeliers caught her just right and he'd realized she was on the verge of tears.

Shimmering tears she never once let fall.

She'd been a beautiful ice queen in the center of that gathering, the most regal and elegant of them all—and he'd wanted to see if he could melt the ice surrounding her heart. Leo lived for challenges, and Anna Constantinides was a challenge. It wasn't simply that he wanted to seduce her. He wanted to make her laugh, wanted to see her eyes light up with pleasure.

Anyone who'd seen the newspapers, who'd

read those ugly headlines and even uglier stories, would know she was suffering. It made him think of another time, another woman, who had also been deeply hurt by what the papers had said about her. His mother had kept the articles from when her affair with Bobby had been splashed through the papers. He'd found them in her personal documents when he was eighteen. She'd been dead for eight years by then.

Until that moment, he'd thought the most devastating thing she'd had in her possession had been the positive paternity test naming Bobby Jackson as his father—a fact Bobby had denied until the test was brought out in court after Leo's mother's death—but the articles had given Leo a whole new level of understanding about what had happened between his parents.

Though Bobby had raised him from the age of ten onward, their relationship could never be termed ordinary. Bobby didn't seem to know how to be a father, either to Leo or his siblings. He tried, but he was more of a dotty uncle than anything.

After Leo found the articles and confronted his father, their relationship had soured. Soon after that, he'd gone to the States to forge his way in business. He'd wanted to prove he didn't need Bobby, or the Jackson name, to succeed. He'd built the Leonidas Group from the ground up, and he'd made more money than Bobby had ever earned, even at the height of his football career.

Since Leo had returned to London recently, he'd been trying damn hard to forge a new relationship with his father. Though it wasn't perfect, they were finally learning to let go of the past and be friends.

Just then, Anna glanced down at her slim gold watch and turned sharply toward him as she realized how long they'd been flying. "Are we lost? Because we should have been there by now."

Leo flexed his fingers on the controls. "We aren't lost, darling. I thought it might be nice to fly for a little while."

He found flying soothing, especially when he wanted to think.

But Anna was used to structure. Her mouth opened. Closed. Opened again. "But why?" she blurted. "There is much to see on Amanti!"

He glanced over at her. Such an uptight woman. He found himself wanting to unpin her hair and see how long it might be. And he definitely wanted to get her out of that bland suit. Grey. Why was the woman wearing grey? The red of her shirt was the only spot of color in her drab outfit. Didn't she know she should be dressed all in red? In vibrant, sassy colors that made the green of her eyes stand out even more than they already did?

She was utterly beautiful, and trying so hard to hide that beauty. He found himself wanting to know why.

"And do you really want to be on Amanti today?" he asked coolly.

Her eyes were wide, her expression haunted. He didn't have to explain what he meant. The newspapers and tabloids couldn't seem to leave the story of Prince Alessandro's surprise engagement alone, especially since he'd picked Allegra Jackson—of those *scandalous* Jacksons—as his bride.

Anna couldn't help but be dragged into the publicity. She was the antithesis of his family, and probably far more suited to being a royal bride by virtue of her lack of scandalous relations.

Which also meant she was the perfect sacrificial lamb for the roasting fires of the papers that dogged the Santinas' every move.

The press loved every minute of her humiliation. Each story that featured Alessandro and Allegra's forbidden love also featured Anna. She endured it with quiet dignity, but Leo wondered how close she was getting to breaking. She was only human after all. It couldn't be easy to see her former fiancé with Allegra.

"I can't hide forever," she said, drawing herself up regally, shuttering her hurt behind her lowered lashes. "The press will have their fun until they tire of the story. If I run away or hide from the world, it will be a thousand times worse."

Her fingers strayed to her neck, caught at her pearls. "No, I have to endure it until it goes away."

Leo swore. He wanted to protect her, and he wanted to shake her at the same time. "It's acceptable to be angry, Anna. And it's acceptable to want to escape."

"I never said I wasn't angry," she snapped before closing her eyes again and saying something in what he assumed was her native Greek. When she trained those green eyes on him again, they were as placid as a secluded lake. She was good. Very good. But he could see the fire she couldn't quite hide in the depths of that gaze. And it pulled at him more than it ought.

"These things pass," she said. "And now we must go to Amanti and begin our tour. The last thing I need is for the press to think I'm off being promiscuous with you."

"Perhaps you need a little promiscuity in your life," he replied, very aware he was being self-serving as he said it. "A little fun that's about you, not about others or what they expect from you."

"You're only saying this because it would suit *your* purposes if I agreed with you. Stop trying to seduce me, Mr. Jackson. It won't work."

It was close to the mark, and inexplicably it made him angry. Except that he wasn't quite sure if it was her or himself he was angry with. He definitely wanted her. She intrigued him. She didn't seem to care who he was or what he offered her—and that made him think of something else, something he'd not let himself consider before. "Were you in love with him?"

Anna spluttered. He loved ruffling her cool, though he hoped the answer was no. For some reason, he needed it to be no.

"That's none of your business! We hardly know each other, Mr. Jackson," she said, her entire body stiff with outrage. Her long fingers gripped the arm of the seat. Her nails were manicured and neat, and there was a pale line on her left ring finger where her engagement ring had once sat. He imagined those elegant fingers playing his body like a fine instrument, and nearly groaned.

Since when was he interested in prim little schoolteachers anyway? Not that Anna was a schoolteacher—she was far too well bred and rich to have an actual job—but she reminded him of one. The kind of teacher who wore buttoned-up suits to work and lacy knickers beneath. Whether she realized it or not, the woman seethed with pent-up sexuality.

Whoever got her to let her hair down and give in to her sensual nature would be one lucky man. He pictured Anna in a bed, her naked body lying against red sheets, those full kissable lips open and eager as he lowered himself onto her and captured her mouth with his own.

Suddenly, flying was getting damned uncomfortable. Leo forced himself to think of something unsexy—like Graziana Ricci's collagen-plumped lips smeared in cherry-red lipstick—and hoped his body would take the hint.

"How can we possibly get to know each other," he said, "if you keep retreating behind that starched formality every time I ask you a question?"

"We don't need to know each other. I'm taking you to Amanti so you can decide whether or not you want to build a hotel there. Beyond that, I'm sure we'll never see each other again. Now, if you will please take us *to* Amanti, we can get on with the tour."

Leo shot her a glance. She was prickly as hell and completely fascinating. "You don't like it when your plans get changed, do you? You're very much a list girl."

Her head whipped around. "A list girl? What, pray tell, is that?"

"You make lists. You like a long list of things to do and then you check them off one by one. There's no room for spontaneity on your lists." He made a checkmark in the air. "Woke up early, check. Ate breakfast, check."

"There's nothing wrong with being organized,

Mr. Jackson," she said. He could hear the starch in her voice, the outrage she tried to keep hidden. She was trying to keep him at a distance, and he wouldn't allow it.

"If you call me Mr. Jackson one more time," he growled, "I'll keep flying until we reach Sicily."

"You wouldn't."

Her arms folded over her prim grey suit, her chin thrusting forward in challenge. Clearly, Anna Constantinides didn't know him very well. No matter how successful he'd become, he'd never shaken that raw, edgy side of his personality that liked to push barriers to their limit. No doubt it came from trying to fit into the Jackson household when he'd been young and motherless and uncertain of his place in their lives. He'd pushed and rebelled, certain his father would throw him out, but Bobby had never wavered in his acceptance once he'd stepped up and admitted paternity.

"I would, in fact," Leo replied. "I've got nothing to lose."

Her jaw clenched tight and he felt suddenly wrong for phrasing it that way. She had everything to lose, or so she thought. A trip to Sicily with him would be devastating in Anna's world. Because she was already the focus of attention and she couldn't fathom drawing yet more. Never mind that if she were only to behave as if she didn't care, the media would soon leave her alone. He knew from experience that they liked nothing better than a victim—and Anna was a perfect victim right now.

"I don't want to go to Sicily, Leo. I want to go to Amanti."

"Tell the truth, Anna. You don't want to do that, either. But you've committed to it and so you want to get there without giving the media anything else to speculate about."

She made a frustrated noise. "Yes. This is precisely the truth. If I could run to Sicily or Egypt or Timbuktu and not have to endure another moment of this shame, I would do it. But I can't run, Leo. I have to carry on as always and wait for the scandal to pass."

It was perhaps the most honest thing she'd said yet. But he wanted more. "Tell me this, then. If you could have an affair, no consequences, no one the wiser, would you do so?"

She didn't say anything for the longest time. "I…I…"

But whatever she was about to say was lost as a light on the instrument panel flashed on. A tight knot formed in Leo's stomach as he turned his focus to the plane. He'd checked everything before they'd left Santa Maria, and everything had been fine. He wouldn't have taken off otherwise.

But something had changed in the half hour since.

CHAPTER THREE

THE plane shuddered and Anna's heart leaped. Whatever she'd been about to say was forgotten as she took in Leo's sudden concentration. "What's happening?"

He didn't look at her. "We're losing fuel pressure," he said as he did something with the switches. The plane shuddered again, and the engine made a high-pitched whining noise that sent her heart into her throat.

"What does that mean?" Because she needed to know, precisely, what he was saying to her. It didn't sound good, and she didn't like the sensation of being out of control. Whatever happened, she was in a plane with Leo, high above the Mediterranean, and there was nothing she could do to fix the problem.

But that didn't mean she intended to sit quietly and hope for the best.

"It means there's a problem in the fuel line. We need to land before we run out of gas."

"Land? Where?" She scanned the horizon, saw nothing but water for kilometers. Her stomach churned. "Leo, there's nothing out here."

He checked the GPS, his long fingers flexing against the controls. "We're too far from Amanti," he finally said, concentrating on the screen. "But there's another island a few miles distant."

Another island? She didn't know what it could be, but she began to pray fervently that they would make it there. The plane bucked again, the engine sputtering before smoothing out once more. Anna gripped her seat, her fingers pressing into the leather so hard that they ached.

"Are we going to die?"

"No." His answer was swift, sure, and she took comfort in it. But doubts began to creep in. What if he was wrong? What if he was only trying to keep her calm? She couldn't abide that. She had to know.

"Tell me the truth, Leo," she finally said, unable to stand it a moment longer. "Please."

Leo's dark eyes glinted with determination as he looked over at her. How could her heart flip at the look on his face when this was serious? How could heat blossom between her thighs at a moment like this?

Because she had regrets, that's why. Because she'd saved herself for years for a husband who had cast her aside before they'd ever even wed.

Now that she might die, she fervently wished she'd experienced passion, even if it had just been for one night.

Leo stared at her so intently that she could almost forget where they were, what was happening. For a moment, she could almost wish they'd had that day in Sicily.

"If we can find this island, we'll be fine," Leo said shortly.

She wanted to believe him, but she couldn't simply accept it without question. "But what if there's nowhere to land?"

"There's definitely somewhere to land," he said. "Look around you."

There was nothing but blue as far as the eye could see. She gasped as she finally took his meaning. "The sea?"

"Yes. Now put on your life jacket, and grab that orange backpack from where it's stowed behind my seat."

"But, Leo," she said, panic rising inside her as she thought of them marooned at sea. Assuming they survived the impact. *Oh, God.*

"Anna, trust me," he said firmly. "Get the pack. Get your life jacket."

"What about you?"

"Grab mine, too. I can't put it on yet, but I will."

Anna unbuckled her seat belt and found the life jackets. She clipped hers on with shaky fingers, and then grabbed the heavy orange pack he'd told her to get and brought everything back to her seat. Leo was saying something into the headset, but he didn't appear to be getting an answer.

"No," he said when she started to sit down again. "Sit in one of the seats behind me. It'll be safer on impact."

Anna hesitated only a moment before sinking into the seat beside him and buckling her seat belt. "I want to be here with you," she said. "I insist on it."

She didn't expect him to laugh, but he did. A short, sharp bark of laughter that stole into her soul and made her feel good, if only for a moment. "Dragon lady," he said, and her heart skipped again. At a time like this, how did he make her feel as if she were formidable? As if she mattered? How did he cut through the pain and anger and make her feel important again?

"There it is," Leo said, and she squinted into the distance, searching the horizon. A small gray bump rose up from the sea, growing bigger the closer they got. There were many small islands out here, some of which were inhabited and some not. Any hope she'd had this might be one of the inhabited ones faded quickly when she saw the size of the island.

It was long, narrow and rocky, with a green

area at one end and a white sandy beach on one side.

"There's nowhere to land," she said.

"I'm taking us down," he replied. "It might be rough."

That was the only warning he gave her as he pointed the nose down and began his descent. Anna's stomach twisted as the plane dropped in the sky. Sweat broke out on her forehead, between her breasts. Her heart went into free fall as the sea grew bigger and bigger with every passing minute.

The engine sputtered and whined, and Leo's hands were white on the controls. But the plane continued to descend in a controlled manner. Anna grasped her pearls in her fingers, twisted hard and then chided herself for doing so. This was no time to break them. They'd been her grandmother's, the only link she had left to the woman she'd most admired. She would not destroy them.

"Leo," she said helplessly as they sank lower in the sky. She reached for him, put her hand on his shoulder, squeezed. She hoped she was imparting strength, courage, but she had the feeling he didn't need any of those things. No, it was she who needed them and Leo who provided them to her.

She could do nothing but sit there and watch

powerlessly as the island got bigger. But the sea was bigger still, so big and azure that it filled her vision from all sides. She focused on the island. There were a few trees, she noted, a wooded copse that might provide shelter—and might have fresh water if the rain had a place to collect. Assuming it rained.

If only they survived the plunge into the sea. *First things first, Anna.* She was so used to planning that she couldn't help herself, when in fact there was nothing to plan if they didn't make it out alive.

"Brace for landing," Leo said as he took the plane dangerously close to the island. Anna closed her eyes at the last minute and gripped her seat for dear life. So many feelings went through her at once that she couldn't process them all. Fear, regret, anger, sadness, love, passion...

Anna's head snapped back as the plane shuddered into the water with a bone-jarring splash. It glided along the surface before coming to an abrupt stop that would have jerked her forward in the seat if not for the belt holding her tightly in place. There was a surreal moment of complete silence as the craft pitched and rolled with the waves. Anna's stomach lodged in her throat. How would they ever escape with the motion throwing them around so much? Once the seat belt was off, two steps forward would turn into four steps back.

"There's not much time," Leo said as he unbuckled his seat belt and flung his door open.

"Your jacket," she said, thrusting it toward him with a shaking hand as she unlocked her seat belt with the other. He took it and threw it out the door, then grabbed her and hauled her toward him. She barely had time to register all the sensations that rocked her as she was pressed against his hard body before she dropped into the sea.

The water was shocking, not because it was too cold, but because it was wet when she'd been so dry. The life preserver kept her from going under, but water still splashed over her head, soaking her. Anna spluttered and began to tread water as Leo landed beside her, the orange pack slung over one shoulder.

"Your life jacket," she said. It was floating just out of reach and she made a grab for it.

"I don't need it." His hair was slicked back from his head, his expression grim and determined.

"Leo," she began.

"I'm fine, Anna. Can you swim to the island?"

She turned and looked at the shore only a few meters distant. "Of course," she said crisply, her heart beating like crazy in her chest as she began to process what had happened. They'd crashed. In the Mediterranean. She couldn't quite wrap her mind around it, and yet the plane bobbed in the water nearby. The scent of salt mingling with jet fuel invaded her senses.

"We need to go now," he said. "Before we get soaked in fuel."

Leo began to stroke toward the island. She followed, easily crossing the distance before stumbling to her knees onto the shore beside him. Her hair was still in its rigid knot, but a few wisps had fallen free and snaked around her neck like tentacles. Her makeup was probably streaked and—

Oh, she'd forgotten her purse! She turned and started wading back into the water when strong arms caught her from behind.

"Where are you going?"

"My purse," she said. "My phone, my identification—"

"It's too late," he growled in her ear.

"But it's not." She pointed. The plane was still on top of the water, though the nose had begun to sink. It wouldn't take her a trifle to get out there and back again.

"It's too dangerous, Anna. Even if the plane wasn't sinking, the remaining fuel is leaching from it. Besides, was there anything irreplaceable in your purse?"

She wanted to tell him yes, of course there was. Instead, Anna slumped in his grip. "No, nothing irreplaceable." Just her lip gloss, her hand sanitizer, her headache tablets and her phone with its calendar of all her events.

Events that were sadly lacking lately. Invitations had dried up since Alex had jilted her.

She stifled a hysterical laugh. They'd crashed in the Mediterranean and she was concerned about her calendar? She needed to be thinking about survival, not social engagements.

Leo held her hard against him. She slowly became aware of his heat, of the solidity of his body where it pressed into hers. They were both soaking wet, dripping onto the sand, and she wondered for a moment why the water didn't sizzle and steam.

Anna put her hand on his where it gripped her beneath the life vest. She wanted to smooth her fingers along his skin, wanted to feel the shape of his hand, the ridges of his knuckles, but instead she loosened his grip and stepped away from him. When she turned, he was looking at her with a kind of laser intensity that made her gut clench in reaction.

Liquid heat flooded her body, her bones. Shakily, she undid the clasp on the vest and shrugged it off. She needed something to do, something that didn't involve looking at Leo.

His shirt was plastered to his chest, delineating every ridge and curve of smooth muscle. She hadn't been able to tell from the tuxedo last night, but Leo was in spectacular shape. His father had once been a famous footballer, she recalled, and Leo looked as if he'd spent quite a bit of time on the field himself. He had the leanly muscled form of an athlete.

"We need to find shelter," he said, and a hard knot formed right below her breastbone. They were stranded, alone, with nothing and no one to help them get home again.

"You were able to tell someone what happened, right?" she said. "They'll be looking for us soon."

His expression remained flat. "We were out of radio range. I activated the emergency beacon on the plane. They'll know approximately where we went down, but it may take some time since they won't be looking for us yet."

She turned back toward the plane. "If I had my mobile phone…"

"Doesn't matter," he said. "There are no cell towers out here. You'd need a satellite phone to make a call."

"So we're stuck."

"For the time being," he replied, hefting the orange pack onto his shoulder again.

"How long will we be here, Leo?"

He shrugged. "I really don't know. Which is why we need to find shelter."

"What about food? Water? How will we survive if we don't have water?"

He gave her a long look. "We have enough water for a couple of days, if we ration it. Everything's in this pack."

Anna blinked. "You have water?"

"It's an emergency survival kit, darling. There's a bit of everything. Dried food, matches, fuel, blankets—enough to survive a few days in the wild."

He turned and started walking toward the other end of the island where she'd seen the copse of trees. Anna scrambled after him. Her feet were bare since she'd lost her shoes in the sea. She felt a momentary pang for the beautiful suede pumps that were no doubt at the bottom of the Med by now, but it was truly the least of her worries.

Part of the going was rocky, but Anna climbed after Leo and never said a word when the rocks sliced into her feet. She fell behind, but she did not call out. Why should she? He couldn't disappear. The island was small and she knew where they were headed. But Leo glanced over his shoulder at one point, stopping when she wasn't right behind him.

He frowned as she approached, his gaze on her feet. "You've lost your shoes."

"They wouldn't have been much use anyway," she said. "They were five-inch platforms."

Her one concession to impracticality.

He closed the distance between them, and then

hooked an arm behind her knees and lifted her into his arms before she realized his plan.

"Leo, put me down!"

His face was close to hers. Too close. Oh, heavens. She wanted to tilt her head back, wanted to nuzzle her face into the crook of his neck and breathe in his scent. And then she wanted to lick him.

Heat flashed through her. The hot Mediterranean sun beat down on them from above, but it wasn't the sun that made her skin prickle or her core melt.

"Once we're over the rocks," he said. "I don't want you cutting your feet."

"Too late," she replied.

His coffee-colored eyes were so beautiful as he stared down at her. There was heat in them, and something darker and more intense. Something so elemental it frightened her. "You should have told me sooner."

"You have the pack," she said, dropping her gaze. Her heart hammered in her breast. Why did he affect her so much? He was completely, utterly wrong for her. He was the kind of man she should definitely avoid, and yet he thrilled her in ways she'd never expected.

He's thrilling because he's dangerous, a voice whispered. *Bad boys are always thrilling.*

"You barely weigh more than the pack does,"

he said. "If it gets too much for me, I'll put one of you down. Honest."

He winked on that last, and began striding toward the trees again. Anna clung to him, ashamed, miserable, grateful and oddly excited. She had to wrap her arms around his neck, had to press her face in close to his. His fingers splayed over her rib cage, dangerously close to her breast, and she held her breath for a long moment.

Would he touch her there? Did she want him to? What would she say if he did?

But they reached a sandy area and he set her down again. She tried not to be disappointed as he strode away. The sand felt good on her feet, warm on top and cool if she dug her toes down. She scrambled after Leo, catching him right as he reached the trees.

It was cooler here, and the ground was flat and somewhat sandy. Leo kept walking until he found a spot he liked, and then he set the pack down and opened it. Anna watched in amazement as he pulled out a variety of items—heavy-duty plastic sheeting with grommets, a knife and rope—before he stood and began to peel the wet shirt from his body.

If she'd thought the navy shirt molded his chest, she'd had no idea what molding meant until he stood there in a wet T-shirt and jeans. But then he yanked the T-shirt off and his chest was bare and tanned. Her gaze dropped, halted in surprise. He had a dragon tattoo low on his abdomen—

Anna gulped. And turned away. Automatically she reached for her pearls, relieved they were still there as her fingers toyed with them.

"Do I make you nervous?" Leo asked from behind her. She could hear the laughter in his voice. Deliberately she turned, dropping her hand away from her neck. *Calm, cool.*

"Of course not," she said.

He winked. "Good. Because I'm afraid the jeans are next, darling. Can't abide wet clothing."

Anna held her breath as his long fingers flicked open the button of his jeans. She couldn't have looked away if her life depended on it. Tanned fingers slipped between the waistband and his skin, and then he was pushing the jeans down. Her heart kicked up as his hip bones appeared, and then the elastic waist of his underwear. Armani, she thought crazily. It said so on the band.

But she forgot all about it as the jeans slid down his long, strong legs, revealing tanned skin and acres of muscle. Anna couldn't breathe. Her lungs simply wouldn't fill. Had she ever seen a man as beautiful, as strong and lean and muscled, as this one?

Could this day be any more surreal? Just a few minutes ago, they'd been fully clothed strangers.

And now they were marooned together and Leo was stripping out of his clothing.

"Keep staring, darling, and the show is bound to get more interesting," Leo said, his voice a growling purr that slid over her nerve endings and made her shudder.

"I've seen naked men before," she said with a sniff. "You can't shock me."

It was only a small lie: the naked man she'd seen had been on a video, not standing before her looking so vibrant and sexy that she physically hurt from looking at him. Leo wasn't wearing any less than a man might wear while swimming, and yet her insides were twisting and squeezing in a way they never had at the sight of a random man in a Speedo at the pool.

"Is that so?" he asked.

"Definitely." But her limbs felt weak.

Leo shook his head, laughing softly. "Come along then, Anna. Get out of your wet things and help me set up this shelter."

Astonishment riveted her to the spot. He wanted her to remove her clothes? She'd not thought of it before, but now it seemed as if her soaked suit clung to her uncomfortably. Her skin felt cool and clammy under the fabric, though Leo's had looked hot and silky when he'd removed his clothing.

Leo strode over to her and began to gently push her jacket from her shoulders. "Come on, Anna, it's all right. You've had a shock. Let's get you out of these wet things. I'll put everything in the sun and it'll be dry again in no time. You can armor yourself behind your buttoned-up clothing quite soon, I promise."

"There's nothing wrong with my clothes," she protested, though she let him tug her jacket down her arms.

"Nothing at all," he agreed.

"Then why did you say it?" She stepped away from him as the jacket fell free and crossed her arms over her breasts. How could she possibly take off her camisole and skirt? How could she stand before him in her bra and panties?

Leo sighed. "Because you're beautiful, Anna. Your clothes should show how beautiful you are, not hide it."

"I'm not hiding anything," she protested, her heart throbbing at the compliment. "My suit is professional, conservative. There's nothing wrong with that."

"No. But I don't think it's really you."

He'd said that to her earlier, and it was no less irritating now. "How can you conceivably think such a thing? We hardly know each other, Mr. Jackson."

She was proud of herself for sounding frosty, though her insides were sizzling hot. Leo was a stunning man and he was standing before her in nothing but a pair of black briefs with a white waistband. He had a dragon tattoo she oddly wanted to press her mouth to. And he'd just told her she was beautiful.

But she knew he didn't mean it—or he did mean it, but the same as he meant it when he'd told whichever woman he'd spent the night with last night that she was beautiful, too. Leo was a playboy, the kind of man who was pretty to look at—and probably amazing to spend the night with—but who had absolutely no intentions beyond a night of pleasure.

He was a glorious, beautiful creature designed for one thing only: to ruin the women he took to his bed. Not ruin in the old-fashioned sense, but ruin in the sense that she couldn't imagine how they ever found another lover to satisfy them once they'd had a taste of him.

Leo snorted. "And when you don't retreat behind clothing, you retreat behind stiff formality. I think we've crossed some sort of barrier that prohibits us from using the terms *mister* and *miss,* don't you?"

"Not at all. Politeness is always acceptable." It was what she'd been taught. Always be gracious, even when you were aching inside. A lady smiled through adversity. A lady didn't let anyone see when she was hurting. A lady never complained.

His snort turned into full-blown laughter. A hot

current of mortification blazed through her at the sound. Why did she say such silly things? Why did she open herself up to his amusement? Leo was the kind of man who said and did what he wanted, and damn the consequences. He couldn't understand her world, couldn't understand why she had to behave stoically and graciously in the face of humiliation.

"Politeness?" he said. "I'm almost naked, darling. And if no one arrives in the next few hours to rescue us, we'll be sharing body heat under a blanket tonight. We've moved far beyond polite, don't you think?"

CHAPTER FOUR

ANNA's heart pounded in her chest. Leo had an edge that both compelled her and frightened her. And when he talked of sharing a blanket—sharing body heat—she began to shiver deep inside.

"If you don't want to be naked when we share that heat, I suggest you take those clothes off and let them dry in the sun."

She didn't want to do so, and yet she knew she had little choice. It was either that or sit in the sun with her clothes on and risk a severe sunburn while she waited for everything to dry. Since her teeth were beginning to chatter, her only option was removal.

Jerkily, her fingers found her zipper and tugged it down. And then she was peeling the skirt from her body, tossing it aside, daring him to say a word as she did so. She almost lost her courage when it came time to remove the camisole, but she told herself it was the same as wearing a bikini—so she peeled the wet camisole upward and shrugged it off.

She looked up then, met Leo's gaze. Realized he hadn't moved since she'd begun to strip. He was staring at her, his dark eyes gleaming hotly. There was something dangerous in his stare, something too intense to fathom. She was perversely happy she'd put on a matching bra and panty set today. They were lacy, pink and not too revealing. *It's a bikini,* she told herself. *A bikini.*

Except that Leo wasn't looking at her like she was wearing a bikini. No, he was looking at her with far more heat and intimacy than if she were dressed in a swimming costume. No man had ever looked at her quite like that before. It was… thrilling. And nerve-racking.

Anna wrapped her arms around her body self-consciously and walked past him to where the pack lay. "Are we building this shelter or not?" she asked crisply, kneeling beside the heavy plastic sheeting. She had to do something, or make an even bigger fool of herself.

She heard him move, and then he reached down and lifted her gently.

"You're cold," he said. And then he pulled her into his embrace, her bare skin coming into heart-stopping contact with his as he pressed her against him, breast to belly to hip.

Her first instinct was to push away, to put as

much distance between them as possible, but he was warm and dry and not the least bit clammy. His heat flowed into her, warmed her cold limbs.

But it was more than that, she realized.

It was sexual heat, embarrassment and longing all rolled into one. Her skin prickled at his nearness. Leo chafed his hands along her arms, her back. For him it was practical while for her…

What an amateur she was! What a pitiful, clueless amateur.

Anna turned her head slightly, breathed in the scent of his skin where her head was pressed to his chest. He smelled like salt, but under that he smelled like soap and spice. She wanted to lick him.

Anna closed her eyes. What was with this constant urge to lick him? Was he an ice cream cone? A lollipop?

Need washed through her, made her knees weak. Thankfully Leo was holding her close, or she'd surely sink to the ground. One hand touched her head, rubbed softly—but no, he wasn't rubbing, he was finding the pins of her knot and pulling them free.

Her hair tumbled loose and she gasped. Automatically she reached up with one hand, wanting to smooth it back into place. But it was a bedraggled rope hanging down her back. No amount of smoothing would help at this point.

She tilted her head back to look up at Leo. His eyes danced with mischief. And something else. Something hot and intense that frightened her as much as it intrigued her. He was a hard man, a ruthless man when he wanted something. She could see that in him, behind the smiles and winks, behind the *darlings*. This was a man who conquered, who took everything and left nothing behind. Would he take her if she allowed it? Would there be anything left when he was done?

Anna shivered again, and not from cold this time. "Why did you do that?" she asked.

"Because your hair will dry faster if you take it down."

Oddly, disappointment spiraled inside her. Part of her had hoped he would say he'd done it because he wanted to see her hair, but of course he was being practical. And yet his eyes darkened, his nostrils flaring as he looked down at her.

His gaze dropped to her lips and her heartbeat slowed to a crawl. He was going to kiss her. She wanted him to kiss her, wanted it almost more than she wanted her next breath. She wanted to feel the heat, the sizzle, the storm of this man's kiss.

But not like this. A thread of panic unwound in her brain. She didn't want her first real kiss to be an afterthought. For him, it was like breathing. For her, it was everything she'd never had.

"No," she said softly as he dipped his head toward hers, her throat aching as she forced the word out.

Leo stopped, straightened. He looked frustrated. Annoyed.

"I've never," she began, trying to explain. "Never…"

She couldn't say it, couldn't admit the shame of never having been kissed. She was twenty-eight years old. She'd been waiting her whole life for a man who had thought less than nothing about rejecting her at the last possible moment. She'd spent years preparing for a wedding that wasn't ever going to happen. Saving herself for a man who didn't want her.

Anger blazed to life like a bonfire. And sadness. She'd missed so much, hadn't she?

"Never what, Anna?"

Her stomach churned. She dropped her head, closed her eyes. "I've never kissed a man before," she said, her voice a husky whisper. Shame clawed into her, singed her with its icy sting. She was a woman who'd never been kissed, who'd never been loved. She was a woman who should have had all those things, and far sooner than now.

Leo went very, very still. She could feel the incredible control he exercised, the restraint, the sudden hum of tension in his body as he stood so still and held her close. "Alessandro never…?"

She shook her head, unable to speak the word. It was humiliating. As if the stories in the papers weren't enough to make her want to hide her head in the sand forever, the secret knowledge that she'd never been kissed properly, never desired, was infinitely worse.

Leo's strong fingers cupped her jaw, tilted her head up. What she saw in his face made her heart squeeze tight. "He was a fool, Anna. Do you understand me? A bloody fool."

And then he pressed his lips to her forehead, gently, sweetly, and she drew in a soft breath laced with tears. A sob hovered in her throat, but she would not let it escape. She barely knew this man, and here she was pressed against him, hot skin to hot skin, her deepest secrets spilling out as if the dam behind which she kept them had suddenly sprung a leak.

Her fingers curled against the hard plane of his chest. He was so warm, so vibrant and alive. She'd never been so close to a man, never felt the things she was feeling right now.

A dagger of need sliced into her. Her sex ached with want. Her nipples were sensitive points against the lace of her bra. Her breasts tingled. She wanted Leo to touch her everywhere. To show her what it meant to make love.

His body was hard against hers. Some parts were harder than others, she realized. His hips pressed into her, his erection unmistakable where it thrust against her belly. A hot, hollow feeling bloomed in her core. If she were an experienced woman, if she'd done this before and knew what she was doing, she'd run her hands over his torso and slide them beneath the waistband of his sexy, sexy underwear.

But she was a virgin, a stupid, insecure virgin, and she was afraid of what she'd never actually done. Afraid of unleashing something she couldn't control, of losing her reason and sanity.

She ached and she wanted and she stood very still while Leo kissed her forehead. And then he took a step back, setting her away from him. His eyes were hotter than she'd ever seen them, and his body...

Oh, heavens, his body was beautiful, his muscles so tense and perfect, his erection now straining against the confines of the briefs.

"Leo..." She didn't know what to say, what to do. She wanted him to do it for her.

But he turned away. "Let's fix this shelter," he said gruffly.

Leo was out of his depth and he wasn't accustomed to it. His usual relationships were simple affairs involving women who knew what they were getting into when they dated him. He was typically monogamous, but serial. His affairs lasted days or weeks or, in some cases, months.

There was no falling in love, no happily ever afters. He didn't believe in them anyway. He'd grown up in Bobby Jackson's household, where his father's relationships with women were anything but normal. Women were the revolving door of Bobby's life. Leo figured it was possible to love one woman forever, but not for a Jackson male. The closest he'd come to a stable relationship was with Jessica Monroe, and that had ended in disaster when she'd wanted more than he could give.

Marriage and children were not for him, and he wouldn't be like Bobby and attempt to do something he was genetically doomed to fail at. The least he could do was spare his nonexistent children the shame of having a Jackson for a father.

Dear God, Anna. She was innocent and incredibly sexy, though she didn't seem to realize it, and Leo wanted her so badly he was having a tough time keeping his body from reacting. He could *not* have her. He reminded himself forcefully of that fact as he glanced over at her. She was too innocent to engage in a torrid affair—to *know* that it was simply an affair.

If he made love to her, she'd want forever. She'd thought that's what she was getting from Prince Alessandro, and she'd happily ordered her life with that end in mind. How could she reformat her thinking simply to gratify Leo's baser urges?

She couldn't, and he wouldn't touch her no matter how he ached.

They'd set up the shelter and he'd gone to lay their clothes in the sun to dry. For once, he prayed they'd be dressed again very soon. Not that he didn't appreciate a gorgeous woman in her underwear, but Anna was so innocent that he felt like a jackass for ogling her. For wanting her.

And he definitely, definitely wanted her. He wanted to fill his hands with her lushness, wanted to slip that lacy pink bra from her shoulders and cup his hands around the mounds of her breasts. He wanted to see the tight points of those nipples he'd felt pressing into him, and then he wanted to fill his senses with her. He wanted to skim his mouth along the sweet skin of her belly and slide her panties from her hips before opening her delicate femininity to his gaze and sliding his tongue along the wet seam of her sex.

He wanted to make Anna come, wanted her to scream his name. He wanted to give her everything she'd missed out on, and he wanted to brand her as his when he did so.

But he couldn't do it. It wasn't fair to her. She was vulnerable and hurting and he couldn't take advantage of her. When he'd thought she was simply an uptight woman who'd been jilted by her fiancé, he'd imagined a bit of sexual fun was exactly what she needed to take her mind off her troubles.

He might be bad, but he wasn't so bad as to seduce an innocent virgin who'd never been kissed before. He had a conscience, no matter if it had often been reported otherwise.

"How long do you think it will take them to find us?" Anna asked, cutting into his thoughts.

He looked over at her and almost wished he hadn't as his gut twisted with longing. Her hair was long, brunette, and she'd finger combed it before it had dried into a tousled, thick mane that suited her far more than her sleek chignons did. He wanted to run his hands through that hair, wanted to bury his fingers in it and tilt her head back while he plundered her mouth with his own.

His body responded in spite of himself, the blood pooling in his groin, filling him. *Ah, damn.* What, was he sixteen again? Unable to exercise even a little bit of control?

Except it wasn't a little control where Anna was concerned, it was a lot. Especially when he could see the raw need shimmering in her eyes.

Leo shrugged casually when he felt anything but casual. "I doubt they'll be looking for us for hours yet."

She frowned. "I was afraid you'd say that."

"We'll be fine, darling," he said lightly. "We have food, water, shelter. All the necessities."

She turned her head away, her hair falling over her shoulder and seemingly caressing one gorgeous breast. He was jealous of her hair at that moment. "That's not what worries me."

It took him a moment to figure out what she meant. At first he thought she meant she was worried to be alone with him, but then he realized it was something far more significant in Anna's world. Something far more insidious. It wasn't being alone with him so much as the perception that being alone with him would create.

"Anna, you can't live your life in fear of what the tabloids will say."

She turned back to him then, her jade-green eyes flashing. "What do you know of it? You're a man, a veritable *god* for all your exploits. I've had nothing but humiliation from them. If they know I'm out here, alone, with you—"

Leo resisted the urge to swear, but barely. "Do you plan to live your entire life by the numbers? Do you think that if only you are good enough, they'll leave you alone?"

She gaped at him. Angry. Fearful. "I…I…"

He wanted to punch something. For her. He wanted her to fight back, wanted her to not give a damn—and he knew he couldn't make her do it. That was his style, not hers. Had his mother given a damn? She must have, since she'd saved the articles. And yet she'd survived it, just as he'd survived the attention later, after her death.

"It doesn't work that way, Anna. Whatever sells magazines or papers is what works. You—and Alessandro and Allegra—are the flavor of the moment. You will *always* be the poor little bride who lost her groom on the eve of the wedding. Always. It's up to you to choose how you deal with it."

She swallowed hard. "How?"

How? It seemed absurd that he was being asked to give advice on dealing with the press since he'd never much cared one way or the other what they'd said about him—since growing up anyway—but he could see she was serious. That she believed he had the answer since his family were in fact a tabloid staple. Thanks to his father.

Bobby didn't care what the press said, so long as they said *something*. His greatest fear, Leo thought, was becoming irrelevant. So long as the media were printing stories, Bobby felt he was doing something right. Even when he'd been in the papers for the wrong reasons—affairs, fights, money trouble, refusing to acknowledge his ten-year-old son until the courts shoved a paternity test in his face. Bobby mined it all and emerged from a pile of excrement smelling like roses.

And yet that wouldn't work for Anna. She

didn't want or need the attention. She didn't crave it.

Leo drew in a breath. He told her the only thing he knew how to tell her. "By being happy. By living your life. By refusing to adhere to some standard you believe some anonymous *they* want from you. You're Anna Constantinides and you're free to be your own person. Screw the press and screw whatever you thought you were supposed to do with your life. The truth, sweet Anna, is that nothing you thought you were going to be is possible any longer."

Her eyes flashed with pain and fury. "I know that."

Leo clenched his fists at his sides to keep from pulling her to him and wrapping her in his embrace. Why did he feel such a strong urge to protect this woman? He wanted her, but that wasn't anything unusual for him. But to shelter her from pain? That was a completely new bit of territory he'd broken, and he still wasn't quite sure how to deal with it.

It must be because of his mother, because he'd never forgotten how she must have kept those articles year after year. Had she reread them? Or had she stashed them away and never looked at them again? He would never know. But he couldn't stand the idea of Anna brooding over what the press said for years to come.

"Then do what you want, Anna," he told her fiercely, trying to impart strength. "Stop trying to please whomever you think it is you must please. Be the dragon lady I know you can be."

She dropped her gaze, studied her feet. Or so it seemed. "My mother is Queen Zoe's best friend. Did you know that?"

He did not. And it made the whole thing seem uglier somehow. "No."

"They've been planning this wedding since we were children. Hoping to unite our families. I have always been Alex's bride, even when I was a six-year-old playing with dolls. It was predestined."

The thought made him angry. Not because he was suddenly judgmental of the way royals ordered their lives, but because someone had told a little girl that this was her destiny and none other would do. She'd never been allowed to choose for herself, never been allowed to grow other than to grow into Prince Alessandro's wife. Everything she'd done had been in preparation for that life. He could see that now.

And it had all come to nothing because Alessandro had met Allegra. Leo loved his sister and wished her all the happiness in the world, but at the moment he was more than furious with Alessandro, a man who'd thought nothing of abandoning his bride-to-be. And he was furious with the Santinas and Constantinideses.

"They were wrong to do that to you, Anna." *All* of them, he silently added. "You should have been allowed to choose for yourself."

She blew out a breath as she combed her fingers through her hair. It was an impossibly sexy gesture. He didn't think she realized it. In fact, he knew she didn't. His groin tightened painfully.

"Perhaps. But it's what I was raised to do. Our mothers planned it when we were toddlers. I've never known quite why, except that I believe my mother and Queen Zoe seemed to think it was the perfect way to ensure the purity of the Santina dynasty."

"The purity? Isn't your father Greek?"

"Yes, but my mother is from Santina originally. Though I don't believe that is the sort of purity they had in mind. It is more of a tradition thing. Someone from another country might not…suit the Santina expectations. They are, as you may have noticed, quite conservative in their thinking. Very traditional. For my parents, it was an honor to have me chosen as the future queen."

"And it never occurred to you to object," he stated.

She shrugged. "Why would it? That was no doubt part of the plan. A girl raised to be a bride, a queen, would not question it, would she?" She shook her head. "Changing everything now—doing what I want to do, as you put it—is a bit like being marooned here with you. Not at all what I expected."

"And did you expect to be here in your knickers?" he teased, though he did not feel like laughing. "What a singular experience, sweet Anna. Think what you will be able to tell your grandchildren."

She looked up sharply, and he wanted to bite his tongue off. Now was not the time to mention progeny to the woman who'd thought she would bear the heir to the throne of Santina some day.

"I think," she said very softly, "that I'll simply see how today goes before I start thinking of the future."

Leo leaned back against a tree trunk and watched her. She was so elegant, so graceful, even in her underwear. She *should* have been a queen. She was the right woman to be a queen. Anger buzzed in his veins like an electrical pulse.

She'd accepted her fate so easily, resigned herself to being a king-in-waiting's future bride. And he suddenly wanted to know if it's what she would have chosen for herself.

"Did you love him, Anna?"

Green eyes brimming with emotion gazed at him steadily. The desire hovering beneath the surface of his psyche flared to life again, its heat scorching and painful. Because it would not be fulfilled. Because he couldn't allow it to be fulfilled.

But Anna pulled at him. Her eyes, her skin, her dark, beautiful hair. Her presence. The wounded woman beneath the buttoned-up suits and dainty femininity drew him in a way that continually surprised him.

He didn't want or need anyone. And yet he wanted *her*. He always got what he wanted because he never gave up until he won. But this time was different. This time, he had to walk away instead of conquer.

"You asked me that already," she said softly. But she didn't look away, didn't dissemble in the way she'd done only a few hours ago.

"And you didn't answer," he replied.

She bit her bottom lip and a shot of lust bolted straight to his groin. *He* wanted to bite that lip. She looked so damn demure in her lacy pink underwear and pearls. Had he ever experienced such a crazy situation in his life? Marooned with a virgin on a deserted island. A virgin who had his libido slipping into overdrive and his body humming with suppressed sexual tension.

"I was," she finally said. "Or I thought I was. When you spend your entire life preparing to marry one person, you start to believe you might love him."

It was an answer, and not an answer. He found it strangely frustrating. "What do you feel now that he's marrying my sister? What bothers you more, the fact you've lost him or the fact the media won't let you forget it?"

She seemed to think about it for a moment before answering. "I thought those feelings were all tangled together, but maybe they aren't. Because I don't hate Allegra, and I don't hate that Alex is marrying her. I hate what it's done to me, how I feel knowing I've wasted so much time preparing for something that won't ever happen."

She shot to her feet then and Leo thought she looked like an Amazon. A petite Amazon, but a fiery one nonetheless. She looked as if she could chew nails for breakfast. He wanted to laugh. Anna was fiery, passionate. She locked it away beneath her suits and her pearls but the woman was a warrior in her soul. A dragon lady.

Her eyes flashed fire. And then she swore long and loud in Greek. Leo leaned back and watched it all happen, amazed and aroused by the display of so much passion. Hell, if she weren't a virgin, they'd burn up together. She'd know what she was getting into and he wouldn't feel in the least bit guilty for taking advantage of her passionate nature.

"I am tired of being the last person everyone thinks about," she said. "I'm tired of doing what's expected of me, of trying so hard to be the best at whatever task I'm given. I'm tired of keeping quiet and bearing it all with a serene smile. I'm tired of following a list of rules that have been drummed into me since I was old enough to talk, and I'm tired of—" here she pressed both hands to her chest "—and I'm tired of being a cold, frigid person that no man wants to touch passionately. I want passion, Leo. I want love and heat and sex. I want it all. And I want it *now*."

CHAPTER FIVE

ANNA'S body was on fire. With fury, with lust, with so many feelings that she couldn't contain them all. He was right, damn him. She didn't really love Alex. She'd thought she had, but she was far angrier over the way she was being portrayed in the media than she was over the fact she would never be the Queen of Santina.

And she was angry with her parents, with the Santinas, because she felt like she'd let them all down by failing to capture Alex's heart when it had never been hers to capture. Not that they'd said anything or chastised her for it, but she felt that way nevertheless. She knew what their hopes had been. Their dreams.

And it was all lying in ruins now.

Alex had never given her a reason to think he loved her, never given her anything beyond the courtesy she'd deserved as his fiancée. He'd never led her to believe there would be love between them.

She'd filled in the blanks on her own. She'd taken his quiet acceptance of their arranged marriage as tacit approval of her and of their future together.

She'd been so blind, so dumb. So damn obedient.

She was through being obedient.

She was through doing what everyone expected.

She was *through*.

Leo was still leaning back against the tree trunk, though he looked anything but casual in that moment. He was watching her with interest. Hot, sharp interest. As if she were a dessert he wanted to devour. As if she were a cold drink of water on a hot day. As if she were a lifeline in a stormy sea.

She was none of those things, but she thrilled to that heated look on his handsome face. She had never, ever been looked at like that before. No man had ever made her tingle like this, or made her limbs soften and ache. She was jumpy, itchy, her skin stretched too tight to contain everything she felt. She would burst with it if she didn't do something soon.

But what? She'd told him she wanted heat and sex and passion right now—and she did, but she was also scared of it. Scared to take the leap and crash and burn instead of soar. It was not like her to leap without a solid plan, without a safety net. It went against everything she'd ever thought about herself.

"Anna," Leo said, his voice edgy and taut.

And she knew then, before she'd even made up her mind about what happened next, he was refusing her. Without another word, without anything else passing between them, she *knew* he was rejecting her. Leo didn't want her. Alex didn't want her. She wasn't desirable, in spite of the way Leo had held her earlier, his body hardening against hers. It had been an illusion, a reaction brought about by proximity and not a true craving.

And the way he'd looked at her just now? Clearly, she was no good at reading the meaning behind his expression. She'd been wrong. Wrong, wrong, wrong.

A fresh wave of humiliation washed over her. Was she truly that clueless? Truly that blind?

Tears of frustration, tears of anger, filled her. And she would rather do anything else than cry in front of this man. She would gut fish for a living before she would let him know how shattered she was by his rejection.

"I can't do this," he said, and the tears pressed hard against her eyes, demanding release. "I can't take advantage of what you offer, no matter how much I might want to."

"Don't," she bit out, her voice sharper than

she'd ever allowed it to be. "For goodness' sake, don't lie to me."

His expression grew stormy. "You think I'm lying about this?"

She laughed, the sound harsh and bitter. "Of course you are! I know who you are, Leo! I have eyes! I saw you this morning—you hadn't even been to bed when I knocked on the door, or at least not to your own bed. When you want a woman, you take her, especially if she offers herself to you." She wrapped her arms around her torso and tilted her chin up. Her lip was trembling badly. "I must conclude then that you do not want *me*."

He swore. "Dammit, you are dense," he grated. "I'm trying to be decent—"

"I don't want you to be decent!" she yelled. "I don't want you *thinking* for me or *telling* me what to do. I'm sick of that, sick of everyone thinking they know what I need more than I do!"

"You're acting on impulse," he growled. "And that's not like you. For pity's sake, *think*. I'm not what you want."

"How dare you," she threw at him. "How absolutely dare you? You're the one who has badgered me since the first moment we met about being my own person, about doing my own thing, about being too uptight and buttoned up and…and… rigid."

"Anna…"

"No," she yelled. "No!" It was too much suddenly. She turned blindly, before the angry tears that hovered on the edge spilled free, and fled toward the sea. It was only a short distance before she was leaping off a small cliff and into the cool blue water. The tiny cuts on her feet burned anew, but she ignored the pain. She'd treated them with antiseptic from Leo's survival kit earlier, and this didn't burn any worse than that had.

She dove down, down, down, testing her lungs, letting them ache before she turned and kicked hard toward the surface. The sun filtered down into the depths, making the water above ripple and sparkle. It was so quiet down here, so peaceful. She could stay down here forever if only it were possible. Down in the depths of the ocean where pain couldn't touch her. Where no one pointed a finger and laughed at her. Where she wasn't pitiful, but isolated from pity.

She kicked again, realizing she'd gone somewhat deeper than she'd first thought she had. The surface wasn't too far, and she wasn't worried about reaching it, but nonetheless a pair of strong arms enclosed around her body and yanked her skyward.

"Are you insane?" Leo demanded when they breeched the surface together. Anna gulped air, the hot burn of it expanding in her lungs. If felt so good to breathe after she'd denied herself for so long. Almost like learning to live when you'd denied yourself the very basics of life—like passion and love and sexual heat.

Anna threw her head back and laughed. This was what it was like to be alive. This…this— rebellion. Yes, by God, *rebellion*. She'd never rebelled in her life, never questioned her fate or her teaching. She'd done everything they asked, been everything they'd told her to be—

And it hadn't been good enough. She'd failed at the one task they'd set for her.

And she didn't care. Dammit, she didn't care! It was liberating not to care.

"Anna!" Leo cried, gripping her shoulders and shaking her hard. They treaded water together, their limbs brushing each other. Each brush was like the stroke of a tiny flame against her skin. His body was hard against hers, his skin hot where the water was cool. He was so very alive, so vibrant, so large and real and *here*.

She wanted to live in the moment for once in her life, wanted to forget about the past, the future, and just *be*.

"Let me go, Leo!" she cried. Because she didn't want to be held against him like this, didn't want the shame of knowing how badly she'd embarrassed herself with him. She'd had enough embarrassment to last her a lifetime. If he let her go, she could float on her back and laugh up at the sun and tell herself she didn't care about anything at all. Not anymore.

"Why did you do that?" Leo demanded. "You could have hurt yourself!"

She slicked her hair back from her face, tilted her chin up defiantly. "Because I *wanted* to. Because I never do what I want. Because I always do what everyone else wants. Now," she said, her jaw tightening. "Let. Me. Go."

Leo's fingers dug into her ribs. It was exciting, thrilling. "Do you have any idea how beautiful you are when you're angry?" he growled.

Her heart skipped a beat. Her stomach clenched tight. "No, don't you dare say that," she lashed out. "You don't want me. You said so."

"I never said that," he grated. "Never. What I don't want is to take advantage of you."

Anna laughed recklessly. "How can you take advantage of me if it's what I want?"

His dark eyes flashed. His hair was slicked to his head, molding the fine shape of his skull. His face was hard, handsome, perfectly beautiful. How had she ever, ever thought Alex handsome when Leo was in the world?

"You aren't thinking like yourself," he said. "You're reacting to everything that's happened. Taking what you offer wouldn't be fair. Have you forgotten that only this morning you refused me?"

Her cheeks burned. No, she hadn't forgotten—

but everything had changed in the space of a few hours. She was tired of being staid, boring Anna. She was ready to be—if only for a little while— exciting Anna who did what she wanted and didn't regret it.

"God, you are arrogant," she breathed. "So certain you know what's right for me. For the world, I'll bet. But you don't, Leo! I will decide what's best for me. From now on, I'll decide. Isn't that what you said? What you told me to do? How can you turn around now and say I'm wrong?"

His expression hardened. His fingers burned into her. His skin was on fire. Her core flooded with heat, her nipples hardening as he brought her closer. They'd drifted toward the rocks, the gray smooth rocks that she'd dived over in her flight. Nearby was a long strip of white sandy beach.

"This is different," he grated.

"Why? Because I'm a virgin? Because you're worried I'll want something from you that you can't give me?"

He looked stunned for a moment, and she knew she'd hit home. It hurt in a way, and it was also liberating. Yes, Leo Jackson, notorious playboy, was afraid that the jilted bride was looking for a replacement husband. How terribly insulting.

It made her feel bold, wild. Reckless in a way she'd never been. She lifted her legs and wrapped them around his torso. His eyes glittered, something very dangerous springing to life in their depths. "You're playing with fire, sweet Anna."

"Maybe I want to get burned." It was the most irresponsible thing she'd ever said, and she felt so free saying it. Defiant.

Leo brought her closer then, his hips flexing against her. Her breath caught, a tiny current of cold fear threatening to douse her in reality. She was indeed playing with fire.

Because he was hard, the ridge of his impressive erection riding against the thin layer of her panties. Anna nearly swallowed her tongue. What was she doing? Was she really so brave? Was she ready for this? Could she abandon herself for a few hours on this island and then go back to Santina—and Amanti—as if nothing had ever happened?

Maybe.

Or maybe not.

But she was determined to find out. They could have died when the plane crashed into the sea. She would have died without knowing passion. That thought more than any other spurred her forward.

"I'm trying to protect you," Leo said, his voice strained and taut. "I'm no good, Anna. I won't offer you forever. You have to know that."

She thought of him this morning in his tux with the pink lipstick on the collar. He was a playboy, a rogue, a man for whom pleasure was a supreme goal. He winked and smiled and charmed, and women fell into his bed.

But maybe that's why he was the right man for this. He knew what he was doing. She was wildly attracted to him. When they were rescued, they would go their separate ways and she could concentrate on building her life anew. With whomever she wanted. However she wanted.

She was free for the first time in her life. Free to make her own choice. And though it was one of the most frightening things she'd ever done, she was choosing Leo. For now.

"Who said anything about forever? I'm asking you for your body, nothing else."

His expression was tortured, even while the flames in the depths of his eyes leaped higher. "Anna," he said gruffly as she flexed her hips against him. Sensation streaked through her at the contact. Oh, if she just kept flexing her hips and rubbing herself against him...

He gripped her waist in his broad hands, and she realized he'd moved them toward the beach and could stand on the bottom now. "You'll regret it," he said. "Today, you might want me, but tomorrow you'll be sorry you gave yourself away to someone who doesn't deserve it. Save yourself for a man who loves you, Anna."

Anna threw her head back and blasted the air with a few choice words in Greek. "Stop trying to save me from myself," she finally said. "I'm a grown woman and it's past time I did what I wanted to do. I've been saving myself for one particular man for years. And it's caused me nothing but grief!"

Leo closed his eyes and muttered a curse. And then he was moving with her, taking them up the beach until he laid her down in the wet sand and came down on top of her. A sliver of excitement ricocheted through her as his body pressed into hers. She tilted her hips up, her sex aching with need as sweet sensation hummed inside her.

"Heaven help me, I can't say no," he told her. "I'm selfish, Anna, and I want what you're offering me. Remember that later."

"I don't care," she whispered.

Leo's eyes were dark, hot and full of promise. Anna was afraid—of course she was!—but she was also ready to live. To do something wholly for herself without regard to what anyone else thought or believed.

He propped himself on an elbow, one hand coming up to stroke the wet skin between her breasts. Water beaded in the trail he left behind. And then he was cupping her jaw, tilting her head back, his head lowering so slowly she thought she might scream.

"I'm going to kiss you, Anna. The way you should have been kissed long before now."

Her eyes fluttered closed, and then Leo's mouth was on hers, his lips full and warm against her own. Anna's heart beat hard as he kissed her. It was a soft kiss, a lovely kiss. Everything she could have hoped for in her first real kiss.

And yet she knew there was more, knew that a kiss could grow wild and needy, and she wanted that. Wanted Leo to kiss her like he was starved for her. She moved beneath him, and he made a noise in his throat that sounded so sexy she wanted to melt.

"Patience," he said against her mouth.

"No," she breathed.

He laughed, and then his tongue touched the seam of her lips. She opened to him, her arms drifting up to wrap around his neck as his tongue plunged into her mouth and tangled with her own.

He tasted like salt and mint and his mouth was hot compared to the coolness of the water. Kissing Leo was a revelation, an unveiling of worlds she'd known existed but had never experienced for herself.

So *this* was what kissing was about. How could your body ache so much from the fusing of mouths? How could you feel so hot and unsettled simply from that one act? How could you want so much more than you'd ever wanted before? How could you feel as if you *needed* more or you would die?

Leo's hand left her jaw, slid down her neck until his fingers spanned her breast. Her nipples were tight points, and he made that sound she loved when he realized it. His thumb teased across her aroused flesh, sending little spikes of pleasure shooting through her body. If she were that sensitive when he touched her through the fabric, what would happen when he removed her bra?

His arousal pressed against her, creating the most delicious sensation whenever either of them moved. She wanted more of that feeling, more of the sensation of spiraling out of control. She wanted it before she started to think too much, before she started to remind herself of all the reasons she shouldn't do this. She was determined to be brave, to do her own thing, but a lifetime of habits didn't cease with one decision.

The kiss grew hotter, Leo demanding more from her, and she answered him eagerly, drinking his kisses as if they were water in the desert. He peeled her bra away from one breast, and then he was kneading her nipple between his thumb and forefinger while she gasped and arched into the caress.

He broke the kiss and bent to her breast, sucking her tight nipple between his lips. The desire was explosive. Every tug of his mouth created an answering spike of pleasure in her sex.

The surf gently rolled in, covering their lower

bodies on every wave, but Anna didn't care if it covered her head so long as Leo never stopped what he was doing. She realized she was clasping him to her, her fingers buried in his lush, dark hair. He peeled the cup from her other breast and sucked that nipple, too, his fingers taking over where his mouth left off on the breast he'd abandoned.

"Leo," she gasped as she tilted her head back in the sand. The sky above was so bright, so blue. The sun was sinking toward the horizon, and dusk wasn't too far away now. No one had come for them—and she was perversely glad.

Abruptly, Leo stood and reached out for her. "Not here," he said.

She took his hand and let him pull her up and lead her toward the shelter. There, he pressed her down onto the survival blanket he'd laid out earlier. The blanket was silver, made of thin thermal sheeting, and Leo paused for a moment, grinning.

"What?" she said, her heart pounding recklessly.

"Gives new meaning to 'served up on a platter.'"

She looked at him quizzically.

"The blanket is silver, like a serving platter. And you are delectable." He came down on top of her, hovering above her body without quite touching her. "And I am a *very* lucky man."

"Leo, please," she said as his mouth dipped to her throat. She wanted more. She wanted more now. Before she let her brain take over and ruin everything.

"All in good time, sweet Anna. But first, I need you to know you can stop this at any time." He gazed down at her, his expression grave, serious, and her heart turned over in her chest. "Just say no, and I'll stop. Got it?"

Anna nodded. She didn't want to say no, and yet she had to acknowledge that she was uncertain enough of herself to possibly do so. Knowing she could was a huge relief.

He bent to kiss her again, his hand burrowing behind her back. A moment later, she felt her bra snap free. For a brief moment she wanted to hug the fabric to her body, to keep herself hidden, but as Leo tugged it up her arms and off, she let go. His remarkable eyes were so dark, so hot, as his gaze slipped over her.

"You are too perfect for words," he said, before he claimed her mouth again.

By slow degrees his kisses grew more heated, more demanding, his tongue sliding against hers in a rhythm that sent pleasure spiking inside her body, inside the aching core of her sex. The fire burned brighter, hotter with every kiss.

She'd never felt like this, never felt this combination of heat and pain that filled her and made her desperate for relief. When would that relief happen? When would he enter her body and take her over the edge?

She craved it. Feared it. Needed it.

But Leo was in no hurry. He worked his way down her body, kissing her skin, licking her the way she'd wanted to lick him, while she squirmed and gasped. Every touch was a revelation. Every stroke of his fingers and tongue on her body only spiraled the need higher until she was ready to beg him.

"Leo," she said urgently.

"Patience, Anna," he said against her skin, the vibration of his voice humming into the deepest recesses of her soul. "I promise you won't regret it."

His mouth trailed over her abdomen, his tongue dipping into her belly button, and then he was sliding her panties from her hips and pushing her legs open for his view. She made a sound of protest, sudden embarrassment scorching her from the inside out. She'd never opened herself to a man, never experienced that moment when his eyes darkened and his jaw hardened—and then his gaze shot to hers, a question in his gorgeous eyes.

"Shall I stop?" he said, and she knew it wasn't an easy thing for him to ask. He sounded tense, edgy. Cautious. And her heart melted.

He looked so beautiful hovering over her, his jaw shadowed with stubble, his dark eyes glittering hot. His erection strained against the fabric of his briefs and she found herself staring at that part of him, wondering how badly this might hurt the first time.

She wouldn't lie to him. "I want to stop," she said softly. His muscles tensed. She knew in that moment he would stand, would walk away and leave her alone if it was what she truly wanted. "But I want to continue even more."

"Oh, Anna," he groaned. And then he bent and kissed her again, his fingers slipping into the slick heat between her legs, his thumb sliding across her clitoris. Sensation crashed through her. She'd done this for herself, of course, but it was different when he was doing it to her. More intense somehow.

His long fingers shaped her sex, caressed every part of it—the plump outer lips, the delicate inner lips, the tiny ridge at the center where all her pleasure was focused. He stroked her again and again, concentrating all his effort on her most sensitive flesh.

Until she came apart with a cry, her body stiffening in his embrace, her legs shaking with the strength of her release.

She moaned, long and loud, and Leo drank her soft moans into his mouth until she stilled.

"Good?"

She closed her eyes, turned her head into her arm and nodded once. Heat flooded her, but was it the heat of her passion or the heat of embarrassment? She didn't know, and she wasn't entirely sure she cared.

Leo toyed with the pearls which still hung around her neck. "It gets better, Anna."

And then he slid down her body and touched his tongue to her sex. "Leo!"

He pushed her legs open, took her with his mouth. She was shocked, and not shocked. She'd watched that video, watched the woman's face as her lover had done exactly this.

It was bliss. Sheer, heart-stopping bliss. Every nerve ending she had was focusing on that one spot, gathering tighter and tighter until she wasn't certain she could take another moment of this sweet torture.

Leo gave her no quarter. He was relentless, flicking his tongue over her still-sensitive skin, licking and sucking her until the tension built so, so impossibly high—

"Leo!" she cried, shattering beneath him, her body shuddering and shuddering until she lay on the blanket, her limbs melting, her body limp. She thought that if she never moved again, if she died here and now, she would be happy.

Her body was dissolving, floating in a void,

and yet she still felt restless and unsatisfied beneath the haze of pleasure. As if she hadn't quite felt everything she could feel yet.

Leo got up and walked away. The glorious heat of him, the flame and passion, was gone. Stunned, she rose up on her elbows, watched him as he stood with his back to her. He didn't move, other than to rake a hand through his hair. Confusion raced through her.

"Leo?"

"We can't go any further," he told her, not turning to look at her. "We can't risk getting you pregnant."

Anna blinked. And then she got to her feet. She was conscious of her nudity, but the sun was sinking low enough that it was darker beneath the trees. And she felt so very, very naughty right now. Confident and beautiful.

Boldly, she went over to stand behind him. She couldn't help but admire his body. He was so very gorgeous, so perfectly made. The muscles in his back bunched and stretched as he pulled his hand through his hair again. She wanted to trace every ridge and swell of him, wanted to spend hours learning his texture.

Leo was so sexy. So male.

So honorable.

Honorable? Not a word she would have associated with Leo before today.

She put a tentative hand on his strong biceps, felt the knot of warm muscle tense beneath her fingertips. Felt the sizzle of current that passed between them. It was odd, this feeling, and yet she was beginning to get used to it. She'd never felt that sizzle with Alex, but maybe that's because she'd always been so rigid around him. So controlled and cool.

She wasn't cool with Leo. Not now anyway.

"It's okay," she said, her heart thudding like mad. "I started the Pill six months ago."

CHAPTER SIX

Leo turned to look at her. His expression was taut, controlled.

She shrugged self-consciously. "I wanted to know Alex a bit better before we had children. I—I know it was my duty, but I wasn't quite ready yet."

It was a small rebellion, but after all these years of waiting and preparing, she wasn't going to get pregnant in the first month and then let Alex walk out of her life. She'd wanted more time. She'd needed to know him better, needed to know who she was as his wife. She'd felt illicit when she'd gone to her doctor to ask for birth control, but she'd always intended to tell Alex she was taking the Pill when they wed. She hadn't meant it to be a secret—but it no longer mattered, did it?

Leo put his hands on her shoulders, breathed out hard. Those clever hands slid down her forearms, leaving a trail of fire as they went. Simply from a caress.

"You plan everything to the letter, don't you?"

She swallowed. "I am a bit obsessive about the details," she said somewhat lightly. But deep down she cringed, waiting for his censure.

Instead, he laughed, a deep sexy sound that thrilled her. "Anna, you are something else."

She tried to frown. "I'm not sure I want to be something else. I want to be interesting. Desirable. Not something else entirely."

He drew her to him. "Oh, you are definitely interesting and desirable. The other was a compliment. I can't remember the last time—"

He stopped speaking abruptly, and she reached up to slide her palm against his face. She couldn't help it. She wanted to touch him. "Can't remember the last time what?"

He shook his head. "Nothing. It's nothing."

And then he was scooping her up and taking her back to the blanket beneath the shelter, laying her down gently, kissing her again and again. The fires in her body stoked higher with every touch of his lips against hers. Leo was still wearing his briefs, and she arched against him in frustration.

"You should know," he said softly against her earlobe as he nibbled her there. "I am healthy. You have nothing to fear. I am always cautious with my…liaisons."

Liaisons. The word lodged in her brain, refused to fade away. She knew Leo had many lovers, knew she was only a *liaison*. This was tempo-rary. It was here, now, a celebration of survival. They would be rescued eventually, she was cer-tain, and they would go back to their lives.

A pang of something pierced her but she dared not examine it.

"Now, Leo," she said as her eyes filled with ri-diculous tears. "Please, now."

Before she changed her mind. Before the fears she'd buried down deep escaped the Pandora's box of her soul. Before boring Anna took over again.

He shrugged out of his briefs, and then she felt him—the hot, hard head of him at her entrance. "Anna," he said, his voice strangled with the con-trol he exercised. "Are you certain?"

She couldn't think. Couldn't speak. Her pulse drummed in her throat, her ears, even the soles of her feet. She was certain, certain...

She pulled his head down to hers and thrust her tongue into his mouth. He moaned softly—and then he moved, thrusting into her body. There was a slight moment of pain before he broke through the barrier, but then he was inside her fully.

Their bodies were joined together more inti-mately than she'd ever imagined. It was odd to feel a man so deep inside her, to feel the throb of his pulse as he held himself very still and kissed her softly.

"Are you okay?" he asked.

Anna wrapped her legs around his hips, knowing instinctively that's what she was supposed to do. "Yes," she breathed. "Oh, yes."

The pain was nothing compared to the pleasure. Finally, she'd done something for herself—she'd made a decision and done what she felt was right for her, not what anyone else wanted her to do. It was exhilarating. So damn exhilarating.

Leo began to move, slowly at first and then more quickly as she caught his rhythm and rose up to meet him over and over again. Her heart swelled with feelings she didn't want to examine, and her body caught the edge of the wave and began to soar further and faster as Leo made love to her.

She had no idea what to expect, but she hadn't quite expected this. This perfect joining of bodies, this sharp edge of feeling, this physical pleasure beyond anything she'd imagined before. She was molten, glowing, burning hotter and hotter with every stroke of his body into hers.

And then she reached the peak of sensation, caught herself on the edge of the precipice, held herself suspended there for what seemed an eternity of the most exquisite pleasure/pain she'd ever known as her body kindled. She was a flash fire, a firecracker waiting to explode.

And then she did explode, soaring over the

edge, free-falling into nothingness as Leo took one stiff nipple into his mouth and suckled hard.

She was aware of Leo following her, of his body pumping into hers harder and faster, of him stiffening and groaning as he spilled inside her.

He swore, hot words that made her sex clench around him. His breathing was hard, but so was hers. He touched his forehead to hers, being very careful not to crush her beneath him.

"That was amazing," he said. "*You* are amazing."

He was still inside her, still hard, and she tilted her hips slightly, wondering if she would feel anything now that it was over. His breath hissed in.

"You want to kill me, don't you?" he said, and she could hear the laugh in his voice.

"Definitely not," she said, feeling more powerful than she ever had before. "I'm not quite finished with you yet."

He did laugh then.

The sun went down and Leo built a small fire near their shelter. They had a lantern for later, but the fire was enough light for now. After he fanned the flames to life, Leo dragged dried food packets out of the survival kit and they had a picnic. They had also gotten dressed again, their clothes having dried in the sun.

Anna was rather disappointed to sit by the fire

with Leo and not be looking at his bare chest, but it was cooler at night and the clothes were definitely needed. She hugged her stiffened jacket around her and glanced over at Leo. Firelight caressed the planes of his face, shadowing his cheeks and the cleft in his chin. Sitting here now, like this, she couldn't believe they'd made love only a short while ago.

She was in some ways a different person than she had been this morning. Oh, not fundamentally different. She was still a nitpicky perfectionist and she still had a desire for order and neatness. Anna sighed. She was also still afraid of looking like a fool in the press, and she still wished she could run away until everything blew over and she ceased being the jilted bride.

But at least she could now say she'd experienced passion. And, oh, what passion. The memory of it made heat flare to life deep in her belly. Leo had initiated her into a world she'd never known. He'd turned her inside out and made her into a raw, needy creature who'd craved his touch.

So much so that she'd begged him to make love to her again soon after the first time. This time, however, he'd rolled onto his back and let her take the lead. She'd been shy at first, afraid, but then she'd discovered how powerful it made her feel when she controlled the pace. Leo was so in charge of his emotions, his reactions—but at one point his head fell back and his eyes closed and he swallowed hard. And that was the moment when triumph swelled in her veins, when she felt her feminine power fully.

Leo looked up then, caught her staring at him. Her first instinct was to glance away, pretend she hadn't been looking, but he smiled and her insides melted. It was so easy being with him like this. Being out here with no one watching, with no fear of prying eyes and lying voices.

Did they even know she was missing yet? Was anyone curious? They knew she'd gone with Leo, so what were they thinking?

Anna frowned. She was pretty sure she knew what they were thinking.

And they weren't wrong, were they? Which was beside the point, because she couldn't really afford for the press to get wind of such an idea. If she was humiliated now, what would happen if they decided to report that she'd spent the night alone on an island with a famous playboy overnight?

"Regrets, Anna?" His voice sliced into her thoughts.

She shook her head. "You?"

"One. That we didn't have a bed."

She shrugged. "I don't mind."

He looked so serious. "You deserved a bed.

Flowers, candles, dinner and hours of kissing first."

She shivered in delight. What would it have been like to go on a real date with Leo? To be wined and dined and made love to in a soft bed with fluffy covers they could snuggle into afterward. "Is that how you usually go about it?"

He frowned then, and she wished she hadn't said it quite like that. Jealous, possessive. A clingy virgin. *Former* virgin.

"I did try to warn you," he said mildly, and yet she got the impression he wasn't in the least bit relaxed when he said it.

She was *not* jealous. Not at all.

It was simply her competitive side coming out, the part of her that always had to be the best at everything. The part that planned and made charts and notes and calendars and felt triumphant when everything came off exactly as she'd envisioned.

There was no chart for this, no plan that would see her through. This thing with Leo simply *was*.

She waved a hand airily, as if it were a trifle. They both knew it was not.

"Forget I said that."

He blew out a breath, and she got the distinct impression he was disappointed. In her. "I wasn't with a woman last night, Anna. I was working on a business deal. When you found me this morning, I'd never actually gone to bed."

Anna's heart pounded. She imagined him at his computer all night. And then, because she couldn't quite help it, she imagined him with a woman, some svelte gorgeous thing who wrapped herself around him and wouldn't let go. She called it being real with herself, when in fact it hurt more than it should.

She knew all about wrapping herself around Leo. She wanted to do it again. She was greedy where he was concerned. She felt such a sense of urgency, as if she needed to experience everything she could in this one night. Before her real life intruded.

"There was lipstick on your collar," she told him matter-of-factly. "Not that I care, of course."

He frowned as he thought about it. Then his expression cleared. "Ah, that would be from the drunk woman who launched herself at me in the men's room of the hotel last night."

Anna blinked, scandalized. She may have acted with complete and utter abandon today, but she was too much of a lady ever to make a fool of herself in public. At least, not on purpose. "And what were you doing that she followed you into the men's room?"

Leo shook his head and laughed. "Mistaken

identity. She was after another fellow, who'd ducked into a stall to hide."

Anna couldn't stifle a giggle. Odd, since she was not ordinarily the giggling sort. "And what happened when she, um, attacked you? Did he come out of hiding?"

"No, the bastard. Fortunately, she passed out before she did too much damage."

"And then what?"

"I carried her to the lobby and informed the staff they would need to see her to her room."

"Oh, my," Anna breathed. "You are quite the white knight."

"I do what I can," he said, that cocky grin of his making her heart twist. For the first time, she thought the grin might actually be genuine and not a part of the armor he wore to hide the darkness within.

"But, Anna," he went on, turning serious. "You don't have to worry about me embarrassing you. When we're back on Santina, we'll do everything properly. I won't see anyone else while we're together."

Her blood beat in her ears. A current of dread uncoiled in her veins. She didn't want to think about Santina, didn't want to think about what would happen when they returned. It was another world, another life, and she didn't want it intruding on her happiness right now. She couldn't think of them there, couldn't imagine him taking her on a date, much less coming home with her for sex.

No, when they got to Santina, it was over. It had to be. Anguish threatened to eat her from the inside out. She wanted to rage that it wasn't fair, that she'd only now allowed herself to be free, but she knew that the fishbowl of her life wouldn't permit her to see Leo once they left the island. She was brave out here where no one could see them. But when she reached home again?

"Let's not talk about that yet," she whispered, gazing into the fire and watching the flames leap and dance. She didn't want to give him up, and yet she had to. For both their sakes. He was Allegra Jackson's brother. What would the media have to say about a romance between the jilted bride and the brother of the new bride? She shuddered to think about it.

It would shame the Santinas. Her parents. And she couldn't do that to them, could she? Not after everything else. They'd counted on her to unite their houses, and she'd failed.

Her parents would be astonished if they could see her now. Horrified. Her mother had often told her when she was a little girl that her impulsiveness would be her downfall if she weren't careful. So she'd always been careful.

Until today.

Leo put a finger under her chin, forced her to

look at him. "Why shouldn't we? I want to see you again, Anna. Not just here, not only like this."

She put her hand on his, gloried in the feel of his skin against hers. A current passed between them, left her aching with renewed want. How much longer did they have together?

"I'm not ready to talk about it. I don't want to spoil anything."

He looked perplexed. "Spoil anything? I'm trying to tell you that I want to see you when we get back. How is that spoiling anything? I *want* to see you, Anna, for as long as we enjoy each other. I thought you'd be delighted."

"Leo, please." She turned her head to the side, pressed a kiss into his palm. He smelled like the smoke from the fire, warm and woodsy, and she closed her eyes to breathe him in deep.

His hand snaked behind her head, drew her toward him. He looked angry, but he was planning to kiss her anyway. A little thrill leaped to life in her belly.

His lips touched hers, softly, lightly. She strained toward him, wanting more, but he withheld himself from her.

"We *will* talk about this," he growled.

"Yes," she breathed, her heart aching. "But not tonight. Please. I don't want to talk about anything tonight. I just want to *feel*."

His breath was warm against her skin as his lips skimmed her jaw. "Fine. Tomorrow, then."

"Thank you."

His voice was a purr against the column of her throat, her jaw. "What do you want from me tonight, sweet Anna?"

Anna hesitated only a moment before she put her hand on his groin, shocking herself with the bold maneuver. But he was hard, ready, and she shivered with anticipation. She ran her fingers along the bulge of his erection, enjoyed it when he sucked in his breath. "You have to ask?"

He smiled against her lips. "I like this side of you," he said, though his voice still contained a note of anger. "It's such a contrast to the buttoned-up side. Rather like a naughty librarian."

A thrill washed through her. "And do you like naughty librarians, Mr. Jackson?"

He kissed her until she couldn't think. "I might."

"What do you do with naughty librarians?" she asked breathlessly, leaning toward him.

"Ah, wouldn't you like to know?"

"I would. I most definitely would."

His hand spread across her thigh, slid upward beneath the hem of her skirt while she held her breath in anticipation. "You enjoy playing with fire, don't you, Anna?" His fingers found her, stroked her over the thin lace of her panties.

"But what happens when you get too close to the flame?"

"Show me," she said on a moan. "I want you to show me."

He did. Thoroughly, completely, devastatingly.

CHAPTER SEVEN

THEY slept entangled in each other's arms, waking when the morning light streamed through the trees and pierced the veil of sleep. They ate food from the packets again, and then Leo took a signal mirror and went out into the sun to send blinding flashes into the sky at regular intervals.

Afterward, they stripped down and went for a swim. Anna could hardly believe she was skinny-dipping with a man, but Leo made her laugh so much when they were together that it all seemed perfectly normal. Who needed schedules or protocol or social engagements when they had this?

And then they made love in a shadowed cove with the water flowing over them and the sun dappling their naked bodies through the rock. Anna had never felt so free or so happy as she did when she was with Leo. He moved inside her so expertly, so beautifully, taking her to the peak again and again before they collapsed to catch their breath. She fell asleep on the beach with Leo holding her close.

"How long was I asleep?" Anna asked when she woke and looked up into his handsome face. He'd been watching her, and she blushed to think that she'd probably snored or looked decidedly unsexy while she'd been sleeping.

"Not long. Twenty minutes or so."

She stretched and yawned. She felt so decadent, so hedonistic. She wasn't wearing a stitch of clothing, and she didn't care. She'd even taken her treasured pearls off, tucking them away with her clothing beneath the shelter. She felt like another woman, lying on the beach with her lover, her body sated, and slightly sore, from his amazing lovemaking. Part of her never wanted to go home again.

"Do you think they'll find us today?" she asked. She almost hoped they didn't, and yet a change of clothing and a hot shower would be welcome. A hot shower with Leo.

No, she couldn't think like that.

He traced a finger over her lips. It was a light caress, nonsexual, and yet her core flooded with renewed heat and moisture. What a revelation it was to be a woman with appetites.

"I don't know," he said. "I hope so. But we have to accept the possibility no one has yet raised the alarm."

"I imagine they would have, since we did not return last night."

He simply looked at her with that combination of sultry and naughty he was so very good at. "You're with me, Anna. No one will be surprised we didn't return."

"Ah," she said, realizing what he meant. That he was Leo Jackson, famous Casanova, and she was a woman who most certainly had been unable to resist his fabled charm. A sliver of helpless anger filtered through her.

And yet it was the truth, wasn't it? She had been unable to resist, like countless other women in his life. In spite of the fact he'd said he wanted to see her when they returned to Santina, she was still only temporary in his life. He wanted her until he tired of her. She was merely another in the parade of women who'd graced his bed.

She'd known it, but it was the one thing she could not be in the real world. The reason this had to end here, on the island, and not later.

"Perhaps now is a good time to talk about what happens when we get back," he said, as if he sensed her turmoil. His dark gaze was so serious and intent as he hovered over her on one elbow.

Anna swallowed, a pang of uneasiness twisting in her stomach. "There's nothing to talk about."

"Nothing at all?" he pressed.

She sighed. "Oh, Leo, you know it won't work."

"Why not? You're a single woman, I'm a single man. Who says we can't see each other?"

She pushed herself upright, turned to look at him. "I can't, Leo. There are…expectations."

He was beginning to look angry. She could see the heat flare to life in his gaze, but it wasn't the kind of heat she liked. It was dark, piercing, scouring her senses. "Expectations? Meaning, I suppose, that I am not quite good enough for those lofty expectations?"

"That's not what I said." The sun had moved higher in the sky now, and the light that had dappled them before was now a strong shaft of sunlight creeping into their cove. Leo's body was golden, hard and lean and perfect. The dragon on his abdomen was fierce, snorting flames that fanned across his hip bone and groin. She'd wanted to trace the line of the dragon with her tongue, but had not been brave enough to do so.

Now, she reached out and traced it with a finger. His muscles clenched beneath her touch. "Where did you get that?"

He caught her hand. "You keep trying to distract me, Anna."

She peered at him from behind lowered lashes. "Is it working?"

"Hardly. Now tell me why we can't see each other on Santina or Amanti or wherever in hell we choose. You aren't marrying Prince Alessandro now. You can do what you want with your life."

She shivered to think so, and yet she knew she had to be careful. She might have been carefree on this island, but she could not afford to be so when they returned. The press would have a field day with this, if they knew, and she refused to be the target of their humiliation any longer. Leo might not be affected by bad press, but she had to live her life the way she always had or be annihilated by it.

"I need time, Leo. I can't just start dating and having affairs. I can't do that to my parents or to the Santinas. Don't you realize what the coverage would be like if we were to start dating? Especially since we seem to have skipped the date part and gone straight to sleeping together? Are you willing to drop me at my door every night with a chaste kiss?"

His eyes flashed. "You are giving them far more power over you than you should." He swore then, shocking words that sounded so coarse and angry coming from his lips. "Why do you care what the headlines say? Don't you know that the true secret to getting them to leave you alone is to do whatever in the hell you want to do? They want a *victim,* Anna—and you have made yourself into a perfect victim."

His words sliced into her, carved themselves into her soul. It hurt. "My reputation—"

"Your reputation," he ground out, "is ruined. You've spent the night on this island alone with me. Once your precious newspapers figure that out, and they will, the headlines about us will make everything up until now seem like a flattering portrayal. You have to show them you don't give a damn what they think."

Her heart throbbed at the anger in his voice. Not only that, but she feared he was right about her reputation. She just had to hope their disappearance together was kept quiet. "It's easy for you, Leo. No one cares that you've slept with your thousandth woman or broken some poor model's heart. They cheer you, applaud you, think you are clever and handsome and fun. But I was supposed to be a queen. They will not be so forgiving of me."

He got to his feet, his body simmering with tension as he looked down at her. "And why do you think you need anyone's forgiveness? You aren't going to *be* a queen, Anna. It's time you stopped acting like you were."

No one came for them that day. Leo signaled with the mirror at regular intervals, but nothing happened. He was tense, angry, and he wasn't quite sure why. It should be so easy, shouldn't it? A beautiful woman who wanted to have hot sex with him and then go their separate ways without any commitment?

He should be ecstatic. It was, after all, his usual modus operandi. He should be buried in her soft, tight body right now, making her moan and scream his name. He should do it as often as they could both tolerate, right up until the minute their rescue arrived. He should, and yet he couldn't.

He was irritated, and that wasn't quite like him. He should be congratulating himself on a lucky escape, but instead he was brooding because the virgin he'd recently bedded only wanted him for sex. And only while they were marooned together.

Pure irony, wasn't it?

He'd never considered that she wouldn't want to see him once they were rescued. No, he'd actually been worried that in spite of her heated pronouncements otherwise, she *would* want more from him. He knew her kind—wide-eyed, idealistic and inexperienced. A sure recipe for disaster in his book.

She was *supposed* to be the kind of woman who wanted forever. She was supposed to want children, a house, a normal family life that included walks in the park, trips to family vacation destinations and a barking dog that tracked mud into the house and shook its wet fur all over the furnishings.

She was supposed to want all the things he didn't, and he was supposed to be the one who pulled back.

But it wasn't happening quite that way, and it disconcerted him more than it should.

He had to admit, the more he thought about it, that it was probably for the best if they didn't see each other again. Less messy for them both if they made a clean break here on the island. If they didn't, Allegra would quite possibly be unhappy with him for dating her husband-to-be's former fiancée. Not that he typically allowed his sister to have a say in his personal life, but for once it would touch her directly.

Because, yes, the press would have a field day with the news. Anna wouldn't like that at all. Neither, he suspected, would Allegra.

The sun dropped behind the horizon and the temperature cooled as storm clouds moved in. They'd hardly spoken in hours when Leo offered Anna another food packet and some water. She looked up at him with those wide green eyes and a jolt of electricity hit him in the gut.

Sex. It was all he could think about when he looked at her, all he wanted.

And all she wanted, if the way she looked at

him was any indication. Like she was starving for something other than food.

He forced himself to turn away. Lightning flashed across the sky in the distance, turning the clouds pink before winking out again. The weather wasn't threatening, but it would probably rain later. Which was a good thing. They were almost out of water, and he'd be able to collect some in the makeshift reservoir he'd created out of plastic sheeting and rocks.

He sat down and they ate in silence as the surf crashed against the beach nearby. It was peaceful out here in a way. So different from his life in London or Los Angeles. There, he was always on the go, always seeking new business opportunities for the Leonidas Group. He traveled and he dated and he moved on to new challenges on a regular basis. Always looking for the next thrill, the next high. It was what he wanted, what he craved.

Anna glanced over at him. He looked up instinctually, as if they were connected on some level he didn't yet understand, and met her gaze. She dropped her chin, stared at the ground.

And then she fixed him with a look. "What did you want to be when you were a child, Leo?"

He didn't attempt to hide the surprise that must have shown on his face. "Where did this come from?"

She shrugged a pretty shoulder. "I'm tired of

the silence. And I want to know," she said, pushing her hair from her face. It was thick hair, long and heavy, and he loved wrapping his hands in it while they made love. When she was on top, her hair flowed around them, curtaining them in their own cocoon. Her green eyes watched him carefully. Coolly, as if she expected rejection and had dared to ask anyway.

He thought about denying her, but strangely he didn't want to. Not yet anyway. "I wanted to be a professional footballer, like my father. His career didn't last long, but the perks did."

"The perks?"

"Women," he said without hesitation, and then felt bad for saying it when she dropped her gaze and swallowed. He'd done it because he was still angry with her, but he wasn't proud of himself for it.

"So why didn't you?" she asked, pressing on.

He finished the packet of dried food and crumpled the foil. What was the point in being an ass? They barely knew each other. They'd had sex—fabulous sex—but they weren't lovers in the usual sense. And they weren't going to be. She'd made that clear.

And Leo Jackson didn't beg.

He didn't need to. Or want to. When they got back to Santina, there would be no shortage of women who wanted his attention. That was the life he was accustomed to, the life he adored. One woman, no matter how sexy, how desirable, wasn't going to change that.

He leaned back on his elbows. "I decided I could make more money catering to the exclusive tastes of the rich and famous. So I did."

"The Leonidas Group."

He could hear the question in her statement.

"Leonidas is my name," he said. He'd hated his name as a child, never understood why his mother had saddled him with something so unwieldy. He'd thought it was because she'd been an heiress and socialite with pretensions beyond her station in life. It wasn't until he was much older that he'd begun to understand she'd wanted him to be strong and brave and fearless.

"Leonidas was a hero king of Sparta," Anna said. "A very brave man."

Leo knew the story by rote. "He led the Greek forces in the Battle of Thermopylae. And he died defending the cause. I prefer to live to fight another day."

"Very sensible of you."

"What about you, Anna?" he asked, wanting to talk about her instead. He didn't like talking about himself. It took him into territory he didn't wish to explore, at least not tonight. He was, quite simply, a man who knew his limitations and hid them behind a strong will to succeed and a wealth of cocky charm he'd inherited from his father. He had no wish to discuss it with her. Or anyone.

But he did want to know what made her tick, who she was in truth. She'd given him glimpses of it last night, today. When she'd been naked beneath him, naked on top of him, surrounding him. She was a passionate woman beneath the uptight exterior. He hated to see that exterior return, and yet he knew it would when their rescue arrived. It was as natural to her as breathing.

"What did you want to be when you were a child? Or was queen your only choice?"

She shook her head. "Oh, no, definitely not. I thought I wanted to be a veterinarian. But then I realized there would be blood, so that idea went away. After that, I wanted to be a celebrity chef for a while. And of course there was the ballerina dream."

"And the princess dream, I imagine."

She tensed. "Of course there was the princess dream. But that one was supposed to come true." She shrugged, yet he knew how difficult it was for her to let the idea be lowered into the ground. "But that is life, yes?"

"Life is many things," Leo said. "Some of them disappointing, some of them frustrating and some of them blissfully happy."

She looked pensive. "Have you ever been blissfully happy?"

He'd opened himself up for that one. "I suppose that depends on how you define happy. But yes, I'd say I have."

If she asked him to name the times, he wasn't sure he could. All he knew was that he must have been very happy at one time or another. He'd lived a hedonistic life. He'd had fun. How could he not have been happy?

He had it all. He had plenty of money and plenty of women. Who needed more?

Anna sighed, the curtain of her hair falling over her forehead as she dipped her chin toward her chest. "I think I'm still waiting for that."

A sharp sensation bloomed in his gut. "Don't wait for it. Make it happen."

She looked up at him, her eyes wide and gleaming in the light of the fire. "I'm trying," she said. "I…" She hesitated before continuing. "It's not that I don't want to see you when we get home again. But I can't. Not yet."

A shaft of lightning lit up the sky, a crack of thunder following hard on its heels. Electricity sizzled in the air. He could smell the sulfur, could feel the bite of it in his throat. It tasted like anger.

"And how long do you think it will take, Anna? One month? Two? Six? A year?"

She swallowed. "I—I don't know."

"Then perhaps you're right," he said tightly. "Perhaps it's best we say goodbye now."

"I knew you'd say that."

Anger whipped through him. "What did you expect me to say? That I'd be happy to wait until you're no longer scared of the media?"

She swallowed. "That's not fair, Leo."

"Nothing ever is," he replied.

The storm broke around midnight. Water poured down onto the plastic sheeting of their makeshift shelter, waking Anna from a deep sleep. Beside her, Leo lay still, one arm propped behind his head as he stared at the roof above their heads. She felt a pang of longing, but shoved it down deep and tried to ignore it. She and Leo were through. And it was best that way.

They lay together beneath the blanket for warmth, but there was no warmth between them. Not any longer.

The thought made a lump form in her throat, a hard heavy knot she couldn't swallow. Tomorrow, perhaps, they would be rescued. And she might never see him again. He was a man of the world, and she was a woman without purpose. She would soon return to her home on Amanti and lock herself away until she could face the world again.

Without Leo. The thought hurt. Crazy.

"Leo," she said—choked, really—and he turned his head toward her. She couldn't stop herself from reaching out and touching his jaw, running her fingers into the silk of his hair.

He stiffened. She expected him to reject her, to push her away, but after a moment he groaned, as if he, too, were unable to stay strong in the face of this overwhelming need.

He caught her hand and pressed a kiss into her palm. Heat flooded her in great waves, softening her limbs, making the ache sharper. He gathered her to him, pulled her into his heat and hardness.

"I want you, Anna. Dammit, I still want you."

"Yes," she breathed. "Oh, yes."

The rain pounded against the sheeting, dripping off the sides, marooning them in a small dry place that became their island within an island. They didn't speak as they stripped and made love. Instead, they spoke in kisses, in touches, in the long luxurious glide of his body into hers. The storm raged around them, between them. Leo managed to take her angrily and tenderly at the same time, and she answered him in kind, their bodies tangling and battling and straining and melting again and again.

When it was over, they collapsed together and slept the night away until they awoke to a bright blue sky, a clean ocean breeze…

…and a boat anchored offshore.

CHAPTER EIGHT

PREGNANT.

Anna stared at the test stick in her fingers, her entire body going hot and cold and numb all at once. She was pregnant. With Leo's child. How had it happened? How could it *possibly* have happened?

She blinked and fell back against the bathroom counter. Oh, God.

No. *No, no, no.*

It had been a month since they'd been rescued from the island. A month since she'd last seen him. As soon as they'd reached Santina, he'd left again. It had broken her heart, but it's what she'd wanted. What she'd insisted on.

She'd returned to her home on Amanti and hidden herself away, waiting for the media attention to die down.

And it had. There'd been a little bit of a stir over their plane crash and subsequent rescue by Santina's coast guard—but then nothing. Alex and

Allegra, and their various siblings, had proven far more interesting to the collective conscious lately, thank goodness.

Leo had gone his merry way, she'd gone hers, and the press had turned their attention to the more flamboyant members of the Jackson family—and even some of the Santinas—and the fallout from the clash of families at the engagement party.

But now...*this*. Oh, God, *this*.

She'd missed Leo. She'd missed his touch, his laugh, his arrogant and cocky grin. She'd missed the feel of his body sliding into hers, the exquisite pleasure he'd given her for two days on that island. She'd missed swimming with him naked, and she'd missed lying beneath a makeshift shelter and making love during a raging storm.

She'd missed everything about being with Leo. But she'd pushed him away, shoved him from her life without so much as a backward glance. It was her fault he was gone.

She looked at the test again, hoping that she'd read it wrong, that the answer had changed somehow. It had not. And she had to tell Leo. He had a right to know. She considered, for one brief moment, terminating the pregnancy.

But she didn't want to. Already, though it frightened her, she loved the idea of a child that was part her and part Leo. How could she not?

She'd felt so adrift recently, but now she felt as if she had a renewed purpose, a reason to be the best person she could be. She would stop feeling sorry for herself and she would teach this baby everything she knew. Her baby would have the freedom to be whatever he or she wanted to be.

From this moment forward, Anna would protect her baby at all costs.

She put the test stick in a drawer. As she was turning away, she caught sight of her reflection in the mirror and stopped short. She looked tired, drawn. Her skin was golden, her eyes bright, but there was a strain in her expression that hadn't been there before. She ran a hand over her cheeks, her forehead. There were circles under her eyes. She'd been so, so tired lately.

Now she knew why she couldn't drag herself out of bed in the morning.

A baby. Leo's baby.

She had to call him. But no, she couldn't just ring him up and deliver news like that over the phone, could she? She had to see him. She had to find out where he was and go to him. She hadn't allowed herself to search for information about him, afraid of what she might find, but now she had no choice.

Anna left the bathroom and went into her huge walk-in closet to retrieve her suitcase. Wherever Leo was, she would find him. And she would tell him personally that he was going to be a father. Her heart leaped at the thought of seeing him again.

But her stomach twisted. She was nervous, stunned. What if he had a girlfriend? What if he didn't want to see her or, worse, didn't care about her news? What then?

Anna tossed a folded sweater set into the suitcase. She couldn't think like that. She simply couldn't. If she did, she'd lose her nerve. And she couldn't lose her nerve. In the not too distant future, she would begin to show. How could she face the media then? How could she shame her parents that way after everything else they'd been through? She would *not* be a laughingstock over this, nor would she allow them to be.

This baby meant too much to her, and she wouldn't allow anyone to make her feel ashamed. But she knew that if she was going to protect her child, she needed Leo.

It only took a matter of hours to make the arrangements, and then she was on her way to London. A check of the newspapers had revealed a photo of Leo just last night in a restaurant with a group of businessmen.

He hadn't been with a woman, and that gave her hope. In fact, when she dared to skim the tabloids from the month since he'd returned to London, she found not one mention of him with another

woman. Perhaps he'd missed her just a little bit.
Perhaps, she thought crazily, he'd even been waiting for her to call him, to tell him she was ready
to see him again. The thought gave her courage.

When her plane touched down at Heathrow,
it was raining heavily. Anna stood in the chilly
London air and hailed a cab to take her to her
hotel. It was no mistake she'd chosen a Leonidas
Group property. The Crescent Hotel was located
in Mayfair, a stunning Victorian-era building that
had been renovated and turned into the kind of
luxury hotel Leo was famous for.

The address was exclusive, the rooms exquisite, and her reception had been beyond compare.
But all she could think about was the owner of the
hotel and what he would say when she told him
her news.

She stood at the window and gazed out over
the view of Hyde Park long after the porter had
delivered her luggage. The park was green, but
the sky was gray and leaden. Black cabs crawled
through the busy streets along with red double-
decker buses and cars of all description. It was
insane compared to Amanti, and she felt a pang
for home. Amanti was modern and busy, but not
as busy as London. This city teemed with people
going about their hectic lives. Lives she didn't understand.

She felt very small and very lost as she watched

the city slide by on the streets below. But she had no time to be lost. She had to find Leo.

His offices weren't very far, so she donned her raincoat and umbrella and followed her phone's GPS directions until she stood outside the tall glass building that housed the Leonidas Group's London headquarters. It had been a bit of a walk from her hotel, but the exercise felt good.

She'd gotten wet during her walk, regardless of the umbrella, and she felt a bit bedraggled and cold, but she would not turn back now. She stood outside the building, staring at the door and trying to gather the courage that had melted on her walk. People streamed by on the sidewalk, oblivious to her torment. The smoky glass of the Leonidas building looked so imposing suddenly, like a black gaping hole into which she would disappear should she be brave enough to enter.

A car pulled up to the curb as Anna stood there, undecided. A moment later, a uniformed driver emerged with an umbrella. He walked past her to the door of the building and waited only a minute before the door swung open and a man came out.

Anna's heart kicked up. A tall, dark-haired man in an expensive suit exited the building. A man she would know anywhere, even were she blindfolded.

A man who was not alone. A fresh chill stole through Anna, rooting her to the spot. The woman with Leo was small, blonde, and clung to his arm as if she'd never let go. She turned her face up to him, smiled, her even white teeth flashing in the semidarkness that was falling on the city.

A hot slice of something passed through Anna then. She almost turned away, almost slunk into the night and back to the hotel. Except she thought of the baby growing inside her—Leo's baby—and courage blazed into her veins again.

"Leo," she said as he passed by.

He ground to a stop as if he'd run into a brick wall. Turned to her, his dark eyes as hot and intense as she remembered them. The woman with him frowned.

"Anna?"

Anna pushed the umbrella back so that her face was no longer shadowed. She was not as beautiful as the woman at his side, not as polished or... as dry, she thought wryly.

"Yes, it's me."

Leo disentangled himself from his companion and came over to her. He was as hard and handsome as always, and her heart skipped a beat at his nearness.

He did not, she noticed, look very friendly as he gazed down at her. She drank in his scent, that unique combination of subtle spice and man that was Leo. She even thought she could smell a tinge of the ocean, of the salt spray against his sun-warmed skin. It took her back so forcefully that she nearly crumpled on the sidewalk in front of him.

He reached out to steady her, and she realized that she'd nearly crumpled in truth, not merely in her head.

"Are you well?" he demanded.

She shook her head, unable to answer for fear of blurting it out right there on the dark street.

Leo swore softly. And then he was gathering her against him, one arm firmly around her, barking orders to his driver and the woman who stood so forlornly under the driver's umbrella. The door to the limo opened, and then Anna was ushered inside the warm interior and Leo slid in beside her. The woman also joined them, Anna noted sourly.

The driver's door shut with a thud and the car sat motionless, idling in the night.

"What are you doing here, Anna?" Leo asked. His voice was hard, cold, unlike the man she'd known on the island. The man who, a moment ago, had gathered her close and put her into the car. For a moment she'd been thrown back to another time. To the tenderness and passion that had flared between them.

She shivered, a long ripple that slid down her spine and over her skin on icy little feet.

"I need to talk to you," she said, turning her

head to look out at the traffic on the street. She could not look at him, or she would crumble. She would blubber everything, regardless of the woman who sat across from them, radiating disapproval and anger.

And that she could not do.

Leo pressed a button and gave his driver instructions, and then they were moving. The woman sat on the seat opposite, arms folded over her ample breasts, jaw set stubbornly as she glared at Anna. Not a business associate, then.

"It's private," Anna added, just in case Leo expected her to say anything with his girlfriend present.

"I gathered," he said shortly.

"Leo," the woman said—whined, really. "You promised you'd take me dancing tonight."

Anna could sense Leo's irritation, even if she couldn't see the expression on his face. "The plan has changed, Donna," he said crisply.

Oddly enough, Anna felt a burst of sympathy for Donna, who seemed to shrink in on herself with Leo's words. It wasn't her fault after all. Donna didn't say another word as the car moved through the city, finally coming to a halt somewhere residential. The door swung open and Leo turned to Anna. "I'll be right back."

He exited the vehicle, held out his hand for Donna, who took it and scooted out the door.

Anna could hear raised voices on the sidewalk. Her skin burned, indignation a hot flush beneath the surface.

Leo had been dating. While she'd shut herself away in Amanti and tried to get over their two days on the island, he'd moved blissfully onward, compelled by the strong sensuality that she knew was as much a part of him as breathing.

Had he done the things to Donna that he'd done to her?

Anger was a cyclone inside her, whirling through her with a force that threatened to split her apart at the seams. It made no sense, since she'd known what he was—*since she'd pushed him away*—but it was true nonetheless.

Leo returned to the car and the door closed behind him. Anna suddenly felt as if she would burst with the fury she felt. It welled inside her with the force of a nuclear reaction. She'd missed him, missed what they'd had, and he'd been with another woman.

She knew it was her fault, knew she'd pushed him away, and yet she couldn't help what happened next, as if it were a chain reaction that had begun the instant he'd walked out of his building with another woman on his arm.

She slapped him.

His head snapped back, the sound like a thunderclap in the quiet car. And then he was glaring at her. She felt wild, dazed, and she lashed out again, an angry sound escaping her as she did so.

This time he caught her wrist in an iron grip. Anna growled, swung with the other hand. It made no sense, but she couldn't stop. He caught that wrist, too, pinned her hard against the seat. And then he was pushing her back, stretching over top of her, pinning her against the seat with his lean, hard-muscled body.

"Did you think I'd be waiting for you, Anna? Is that why you're angry?"

"Let me go," she said, her voice as cold as she could make it. And yet a part of her thrilled at his touch. Her core softened, her body aching for his possession once more. Liquid heat flooded her sex.

He was so close. Too close. His breath fanned across her cheek. "I'm afraid not, darling. I'd rather like to keep my head attached to my shoulders."

Her breath hissed in as he moved against her, so warm and hard and familiar. Anna closed her eyes as a sob built inside her chest. She couldn't want him, not like this. How could she let herself feel this way? How could she want him inside her again, possessing her, making her his in a way no man ever had before? One month since they'd been together, and he'd forgotten her so easily.

What did you expect? You pushed him away.

Anna bit down on the angry tears that threatened to spill free. She'd done what was necessary, and she'd thought of him almost nonstop since. He clearly hadn't had the same problem.

She started to struggle, her body twisting beneath him. A sob broke free as he deflected the knee she'd aimed at his balls.

"Dammit, what is the matter with you?" he growled.

"You," she choked out. "You're a bastard."

She could feel the leashed violence in him. "I am, in fact," he said coldly. "But I doubt my birth is what you've come to discuss."

She lay against the seat, her body trembling beneath his, his heat soaking into her, warming her. Perversely, she wanted to turn her face into his neck, wanted to nibble the skin there.

She would not.

"What do you want, Anna?" Leo demanded. "Why did you come here?"

It was all wrong. Everything she'd wanted to say, wanted to tell him. This wasn't the way it was supposed to happen. He was supposed to be happy to see her again. He was supposed to want her, and she was supposed to be the strong one, the one who pushed him away. As she'd done on the island. She was supposed to tell him in a dignified tone that she was expecting his child.

He was supposed to be grateful she'd returned to his life.

Grateful?

Heavens above, this man was anything but happy to see her. He would be anything but grateful. How could she tell him?

How could she not?

"Not like this," she said. Whimpered, actually.

His grip on her wrists tightened until she nearly cried out in pain, but he released her and shoved back away from her. Then he was pushing his hand through his hair and cursing softly.

Anna sat up. Straightened her damp trousers. Fiddled with the cuffs of her raincoat. All the while breathing deeply, telling herself she would not cry. She'd survived Alex Santina—she could certainly survive Leo! Alex hadn't meant anything to her, but his betrayal had been far more humiliating.

Leo was the man she'd given herself to, the man she'd bared her soul to—and the man she'd pushed from her life. Could she blame him for being so angry with her, so cold?

"Where are you staying?" he demanded in clipped tones.

"The Crescent," she shot back.

"Ah," he said.

Heat flared to life inside her. "And what is wrong with that?"

"Nothing," he said a moment later. He gave instructions to the driver and the car slipped into traffic again.

They rode in silence for some time, until the feelings knotting in her belly demanded release. "It didn't take you very long, did it?"

His head swung toward her. "I beg your pardon?"

"You know what I mean, Leo. The woman. Donna. Is she the first?"

She could feel him stiffen beside her. "If I recall correctly, you're the one who said a relationship between us was impossible."

Shame roiled inside her. "You know why."

"I know why you believed it to be true. Have you changed your mind, sweet Anna? Is that why you're here?"

Her skin prickled at the name he used. He'd called her that on the island, and while she knew it had first been done in jest, it had come to mean so much more in the two days they'd shared.

It meant nothing now.

How had she let this happen? How had she lost her sense of right and wrong in so brief a time on the island? She'd been weak, and she'd allowed him inside the walls she'd erected. She'd wanted to be close to someone, and he'd offered her that. She'd known better, but she'd been weak.

"No," she breathed, unable to say anything else.

But it was a lie. Because she needed him if she were to have this baby and keep scandal from raining down on her head—their heads—like hellfire. She would endure whatever she had to endure for herself, but for her baby she would fight tooth and nail to provide the happiest, safest environment possible. And she needed Leo to help her do it.

"Then what is there to say?" he demanded. "Surely you have not come all this way to see if I have moved on with my life."

Anna folded her arms over her breasts. Her body was trembling, but whether from anger or cold she wasn't certain. "Which wasn't so very hard to do, was it?"

Yes, it stung, and yes, she knew she had no right to be hurt. It didn't change the way she felt seeing him with another woman, however. She'd felt as if someone had reached inside her and ripped her heart from her body. It stunned her, and worried her.

Leo swore. She didn't blame him. "You can't have it both ways, Anna. You might sit in your cold lonely house and congratulate yourself on avoiding another scandal, but you can't expect others to do the same."

"I don't," she said softly.

They traveled in silence for several minutes, the air as crisp and electrical as if a lightning strike had occurred in the center of the car. Anna's throat hurt from the giant lump that wouldn't let her speak the words she needed to say. Leo didn't make it easy on her, either. He sat with his fingers drumming the armrest, his face turned away from her to look out the window. He was so remote, so distant, and she didn't know how to breach that distance. How to say what she had to say.

She'd had no trouble breaching the distance between them on the island, but they'd been stripped to their barest elements there, incapable of erecting the walls that now separated them from each other. These walls were seemingly insurmountable, and yet she had to find a way.

The car pulled to a halt beneath a bright red awning, and she realized they'd reached the Crescent Hotel. Her heartbeat sped up as the uniformed doorman came down the stairs and reached for the car door.

Leo turned to her, his eyes glittering, his jaw hard. He looked so cold and remote, so untouchable, and her stomach knotted in panic.

"Unless you have something you wish to say, I'll say good-night now."

"So you can return to Donna?" she lashed out.

"You assured me this was the way you wanted it, Anna."

Where had he gone, that man who'd been so fierce and tender on the island? In spite of her wish to be strong, a single tear slid down her cheek.

"Something has changed," she said, pushing the words past her aching throat.

He clenched the fingers of one hand in his lap. She sensed that he had grown very, very still. Waiting for her to continue. Waiting for that moment when she would speak the words that would change everything. Did he know what it was? Did he suspect? Or did he simply think she was crazy?

The door swung open, the sounds from the street suddenly louder. The scent of some kind of food on the wind—an Indian curry, perhaps—skated inside the car, made her press a sudden hand to her mouth.

"Anna?" He still sounded cold and distant compared to the island—and yet his hard veneer seemed to crack just a shade.

It wasn't much, but it was enough to give her the sliver of courage she needed. Her heart thudded, her stomach twisting in fear. She rubbed damp palms along the fine weave of her trench coat.

And then the words fell from her mouth as if they'd been hovering there all along.

"I'm pregnant, Leo."

CHAPTER NINE

HE HADN'T heard her correctly. Surely he hadn't. The world seemed to slow, the sounds from outside the car distorting in his ears like he was on a carnival ride. Leo could only focus on her, on her tired face and huge eyes. Her long hair was twisted up high on her head, as always, and she wore the pearls she'd had on the island. Her white raincoat stood out starkly in the dark interior of the car, contrasted with the black V-neck sweater and trousers she wore.

No color, as usual. Anna didn't like color.

"How?" he asked, his voice colder than he wanted it to be. Shocked.

She looked away. Shrugged. "I don't know. I—I was on the Pill, but of course I didn't have it for the two days we were marooned." Her chin dropped to her chest. "I might have messed up the dosage after we returned."

She fingered her pearls, a nervous gesture he knew all too well.

Leo could only blink. A current of ice flowed through him, freezing him to the spot. A baby. His baby. He had no doubt the baby was his. No doubt.

But he couldn't be a father. He was the last person in the world fit to be a father. What if he was too much like Bobby? What if he didn't know what to do when this tiny being came into the world and needed him?

Panic threaded through the ice, melting his immobility. He exited the car smoothly and held out his hand for her. After a brief hesitation, she slipped her fingers into his palm. Fresh sensation rocked him at the touch of her skin on his.

She didn't say anything as he led her inside the hotel and over to the brass-and-wood lift. "Which room?" he asked as the lift operator waited patiently.

"Five-oh-four," she said quietly.

The lift began to move, its speed belying its age as they reached the fifth floor very quickly. "Here you are, Mr. Jackson," the operator said.

Leo took a bank note from his breast pocket and shoved it into the man's hand, uncaring how much it was for, and escorted Anna down the hall to her room. She fished the key card from her pocket, and then he opened the door and let her pass through before he closed it behind him and took a deep breath.

Pregnant.

A lamp burned in the suite, illuminating the sitting area. The room was furnished with the finest antiques, the best silks, the latest electronics—but Leo could focus on none of those things. All he could see was the woman standing across from him. Her raincoat was still buttoned up, her hands shoved in the pockets. Her eyes said she was tired, worn, wary.

Fury burned through him. She was afraid of him? Of *him?* After all they'd been through together?

"You have confirmed this pregnancy?" he said. It wasn't the first time a woman had claimed to be having his baby, though it was the first time he thought it was true.

Her head snapped up, her chin thrusting forward defiantly. "I only took the test this morning. It was positive."

"You have not been to a doctor?"

She shook her head. "I…I panicked. I had to see you."

"And what is your plan now, Anna? What do you want from me?" He knew he sounded callous and cruel, but he couldn't seem to quite wrap his head around the fact he'd fathered a child. An innocent child who deserved far better than Leo could give. "If you are considering terminating the pregnancy, I won't interfere," he added.

Her jaw dropped, her eyes growing wide. She clutched a hand over her stomach, and he felt like an ass.

"I'm not," she said firmly. "I want this baby."

"Why?" He didn't mean to be cruel, but he had to know. His mother had been a single parent up until her death. He'd often wondered if she would have chosen differently if she'd realized how difficult it would be.

"Because I do. Because I'm not without means, and because I'm not so selfish as to deny this baby a chance at life when I have so much to give."

"It won't be easy," he said. "You have to know that."

She looked determined. Fiery. *Dragon lady*.

"I am well aware."

Leo walked over to the stocked liquor cabinet and poured two fingers of Scotch. He needed something to calm the rat-a-tat-tat of his heart, something to ease the jangle of shock coursing through him. *Pregnant*.

He'd always been so cautious. No doubt it was because of the circumstances of his birth— something he swore he would never do to his own child. Leo hadn't even known, until he was ten years old and motherless, that he actually *had* a father.

He lifted the crystal tumbler. The first sip of

liquid scalded his throat, his gut. He welcomed it. Needed it. Craved it.

"I will support you and the child, of course," he said, turning back to her. Because he would not abandon his child. He would do the best he could, though he had no idea just yet what his best was.

"We don't need your support," she shot back, head held high. He knew she was still offended that he'd said he wouldn't stand in the way of a termination. But he'd had no idea what else to say. He didn't know how to be a father. In fact, he didn't know what he felt about anything at this moment. "Money is not the issue."

"No, of course not," he said. Anna came from money, and she had an inheritance of her own—rather like his mother had had. But his mother's money hadn't protected her in the end. She'd still died alone, and she'd left him to the care of a father he'd never known existed until she was gone. What a shock that had been, going from one household to another in a matter of weeks. From one loving parent to the other who was a stranger.

Leo knew in his mind where this conversation was leading, where he had to take it, and yet part of him resisted doing so. He sipped the Scotch as if he were savoring the last moments of his freedom.

"I need something else from you," she said, her

accent growing heavier with the emotion she was feeling. "Something other than money."

He thought for one terrifying moment that she would sink to her knees and beg, but of course she didn't. This was Anna.

She lifted her head higher, if that were possible, her eyes gleaming with determination. With fire. A bolt of desire shot through him, reminded him forcefully of why he'd wanted her in the first place.

"And what is that, sweet Anna?" But he already knew what she would say before she said it. Because he knew her. Knew what drove her.

The words fell from her lips exactly as he expected they would. "I need your name."

He didn't speak, and she wondered if he'd heard her. He looked so distant, so detached. And so gorgeously male she wanted to weep. He wore a dark suit, custom fit, of course. He wore no tie, but a deep blue shirt open at the neck. He looked like the ladies' man he was, she thought bitterly. His dark hair was combed back from his face, the ends curling up over his collar in sexy little waves she wanted to touch. His perfect face was serious, troubled. Not at all the carefree playboy he was reputed to be.

He cradled the crystal tumbler in one hand, stared at the contents before turning it up and draining it. "Are you asking me to marry you, sweet Anna?" he said, his voice deceptively mild.

Anna swallowed. "Yes." Because it was the best way, the only way, to protect their child. She'd thought about it a lot on the flight today, and she'd known it was right. "But don't fear I mean to tie you down," she continued. "The marriage will be temporary."

One dark eyebrow arched. "Temporary?"

She could hear the ice in his voice, the disdain, but she hurried on anyway. "It makes the most sense. We marry to give our child a name." She licked her lips. "To prevent any scandal…and—and then we divorce after the baby is born. The perfect solution."

"Of course," he said coolly.

She twisted her fingers together in front of her, realized it made her seem uncertain. She made a deliberate effort to stop. To remove her trench coat calmly and lay it across the back of a leather chair. To sink onto the overstuffed couch and lean back against the cushions. To tilt her head up to watch him with what she hoped was a competent and serene expression on her face.

"I'm glad you see it my way," she said.

He set the tumbler down on the bar, stalked across the room like a caged lion suddenly unleashed. "Did I say that?" His voice was so sharp it could cut glass. Cold. Full of thinly veiled rage.

Anna shivered involuntarily. She was tired, and her heart slammed against her ribs. She hadn't eaten a thing all day. She wanted to curl up and go to sleep for hours, and she wanted to wake up and have Leo by her side. Smiling down at her as he brushed the hair from her face and kissed her. Just like on the island.

"You have an alternative plan?" she asked. She sounded so businesslike when in fact she wasn't businesslike at all. Her insides were clenching tight and a tiny muscle in her throat began to throb.

"You've not really thought this through, have you, Anna?"

"I did," she said. "I considered alternatives. This is the best choice."

"For whom?"

She blinked, momentarily disconcerted by the question. "F-for us. For our child. Would you have him or her born under a cloud of scandal?"

A muscle in his cheek flexed. "I think, darling, you are the only one who cares about that. There are worse ways to begin life."

Anna pressed a hand to her belly self-consciously. A current of anger whipped up like a mini dust storm inside her. "You know why it's important to me!"

Hot tears pressed against her eyes. The insanity had calmed a bit since Alex had jilted her over a month ago now, but she knew she was still an object of interest. If she gave the press something scandalous to report, she'd be back in the headlines in what she'd once heard referred to as a New York minute. Which she took to mean blindingly fast.

Leo was still remote and cool. "I know why it's important to you. I simply don't understand why you care. And I don't think you've thought this completely through, Anna."

She sniffed. "Then tell me what I've forgotten."

He came over and put a hand on the couch on either side of her head, trapping her in the circle of his arms. She would have ducked away, but she wouldn't let him know how much he still affected her. Not after Donna. Let him think she was unmoved by him.

Anna tilted her head back while he bent until his face was only inches from hers. She could see the bulge of muscle in his upper arms, the stretch of expensive fabric across his chest. The blue shirt gaped open, revealing tanned skin that had once pressed so sensually against her own.

"You're here, with me, in one of my hotel rooms. You jumped on a plane, without warning, and flew to London to be with me. You had no prior plans to come, you simply leaped without thinking."

"It wasn't like that," she gasped—and yet she

knew very well that it was. From the moment she'd seen the two pink lines on the test, she hadn't been thinking clearly. Coherently. She'd simply known she had to see Leo, had to tell him what they'd created together.

"And yet that's what it looks like. If we marry—and I assume you want it to happen quickly—what do you think your precious media will say then? They will put two and two together, don't you think?"

Anna dropped her gaze from his. "It's possible." And then, because she couldn't help herself, she reached up and cupped his face in both hands, her fingers shaking as she spread them over the blades of his cheekbones. She thought he shuddered at her touch, but she couldn't be sure. She didn't have time to be sure. "But, Leo, it won't matter once we marry. It will be nothing more than speculation, and our baby will be safe."

His gaze dropped to her mouth, his lashes dipping over the hot gleam in those dark eyes. A shot of pure lust hurtled to her core. In spite of being tired, in spite of being pregnant, in spite of the pain and anger of seeing him again, her body wanted his. Ached for his.

It was outrageous—and inevitable, she realized. Hadn't she secretly gloried in the idea she would soon be at his side on the long trip to London?

A healthy dose of self-disgust filled her. Was

she truly that weak and susceptible? She let her hands fall away from his face. He pushed upright again, the moment broken in ways she didn't understand. What had there been to break?

And yet, looking at the hard angry glint in his gaze, she knew there had been something after all. Regret sliced deep, but she pushed it away. She had no time to puzzle it out. She needed to convince him to marry her and let the rest sort itself out later.

"I should send you home," he said. "Back to your miserable existence."

"But you won't." She was confident he wouldn't. She didn't know why, but she just knew he would *not* send her away. She could feel it in the way he looked at her, in the recognition that flowed between them. They were in this together, like it or not.

He shook his head slowly. "No, I won't. I'll do something far worse."

Her heart skipped a beat. What could be worse than going home to face the media frenzy alone? But she didn't speak. She simply waited.

"I'll marry you, Anna," Leo said softly. "But not on your terms, darling."

Fear spiked, twisting her stomach. "I—I didn't think I offered terms. I simply said it would be temporary."

His smile managed to both chill her and thrill

her at the same time. "Temporary implies this would be a false marriage. A pretend marriage. And I won't pretend, Anna. I'm not going to. So if you want this marriage, then know you'll be sharing my bed and my life for as long as it lasts."

Horror seeped into her bones. "But that—" She stopped, swallowed. This was not at all what she'd imagined. She'd imagined a nice, tidy little arrangement that gave her baby a name and had them acting together toward one purpose. Naively, she'd even thought that after a couple of weeks together, they could live apart the majority of the time. Certainly Leo's schedule as a busy entrepreneur would make that possible.

But this…oh, heavens. "That's blackmail," she said, her throat constricting around the words. "You know I have no choice but to accept whatever conditions you attach."

His gaze glittered. "You always have a choice."

Not if she wanted to protect her baby. "Why are you doing this? Why can't we just be civil about it? I've not asked for much from you. Just that you do the right thing and help me protect our child from the scandal that will surely break if I remain unwed." Her voice had risen until she was practically shouting.

Leo was unmoved. He stared at her coldly. "Are you quite finished?"

"For the moment," she said defiantly. Damn

him for making her so emotional! Damn him for standing there and looking so unruffled, so cold, while she was a mess of feelings and insecurities. Nothing touched him.

"Have you ever considered," he said, "that perhaps you are more worried about yourself than you are about the child? Do you honestly believe that it will matter in five years—or ten or twenty—whether or not you were married when you gave birth? Do you think a child cares more for your marital status than whether or not he has a happy and safe home to grow up in?"

Anna swallowed as a tiny sliver of doubt pricked her. There was something in his voice that cut deep. *Was* she more concerned about herself? Was she too afraid to face the fire alone?

"Leo, I—"

He held up a hand, silencing her. "We will marry, Anna. But on my terms. If you can't live with those terms, you *do* have a choice. If you don't make that choice, then don't blame me for your own cowardice."

By the time Leo made it back to his temporary lodgings—Bobby's Knightsbridge apartment—the shock of what had happened tonight was pressing hard against the confines of his head, making his temples throb. He'd gone from bachelor to expectant father in the space of a breath, and now he was getting married.

Married. The second thing he felt completely unqualified to do, fatherhood being the first. And he'd not started this marriage-to-be off on quite the right footing, had he? But he'd been so bloody angry with her, with her plans and schemes. She was having his child and she still thought of him as an accessory. A temporary inconvenience. A sperm donor she only needed for a short while to stave off scandal.

It infuriated him. And yes, it hurt deep down on a level that surprised him. He knew he wasn't fit to be a father, thanks to his genetic material, but she only assumed it to be true. And only on the barest of evidence.

Leo stepped into the private elevator that awaited him. He wasn't accustomed to not being in control of the situation. *He* was the one who made decisions, who made things happen. He wasn't an accessory, and he damn sure wasn't going to be an ornamental husband simply to please her.

Because the one thing he'd realized tonight when she'd landed so forcefully back into his life was that he still wanted her. One brief touch of her skin against his on the street, the scent of her sweet perfume filling his nostrils, and he'd been harder than stone. She'd managed in two seconds what no woman since he'd left the island had managed at all. If he was going to be married to her, then dammit, he was going to enjoy it.

Leo froze as the elevator doors opened onto the foyer of the apartment.

The television blared from the living area, which meant that Bobby had stopped by again. Bobby often let himself in when Leo wasn't home. Since he'd returned to London, his father had come around a lot, almost as if he'd missed Leo over the years. Their relationship had never been much of a father-son relationship, but one of the things Leo had been determined to do when he returned to London was put his anger at his father behind him.

It wasn't always easy, but it was getting easier with time.

Leo had intended to stay in one of his hotels until he found the right place to buy, but Bobby had insisted he stay in the apartment since Bobby rarely used it anymore. Leo had wanted to refuse, but one look at the hopeful expression on his father's face and he'd been unable to do it.

"He's missed you, Leo," Allegra had said.

"Did he say that?" Leo had practically snapped.

His sister had shook her head. She was the good girl in the family, the sweet one who tried to keep peace between them all. "Not in so many words. But he did. He's talked of nothing else since you said you were coming back again."

Leo sighed. Bobby wasn't a bad man; he was simply an impulsive and irresponsible one.

The last person Leo felt like dealing with tonight was Bobby, but he threw his jacket across a chair and headed into the lounge anyway. Bobby was watching a football game and drinking a beer, shouting when his favorite player made a particularly tricky shot. The ball missed the net and Bobby swore.

"Hey, Leo," he said, looking up when the shadow of Leo's form fell across the room.

Leo shoved both hands into his pockets. "Dad."

"Something wrong, boy?" Bobby asked, muting the television as he gazed up at Leo. Somehow, Leo wasn't surprised his turmoil was showing. He *was* surprised that Bobby asked about it, however.

Yes, he wanted to say. *Help me figure this out. Tell me something useful.*

"Nothing I can't handle," he replied instead. He'd learned long ago not to count on Bobby for advice. Bobby meant well, but he had no clue. Like when he'd stood up at Allegra's engagement party and congratulated her on landing a wealthy prince. That had certainly *not* been his finest moment.

Bobby shrugged. "You always were a smart

kid. Got that from your mother. I'm right proud of you, you know."

Leo felt a twinge of hurt at the mention of his mother. Bobby had long ago apologized for the way he'd left Leo's mother to raise him alone, but it still hurt sometimes when Bobby mentioned her. "Yeah. Thanks."

His father looked up again, his forehead creasing. "You want me to go?"

He did—and he didn't. "Not if you don't want to."

Bobby leaned back on the couch and took another sip of beer. "Chantelle's having some damn girls' night thing at home and I didn't want to be around for it. Women can be diabolical when they congregate in packs, let me tell you."

Leo went into the kitchen and grabbed a beer of his own before returning and sitting across from Bobby. The game continued unabated, Bobby cursing and cheering depending on who was down at the time.

Leo drank his beer, feeling sour. Why hadn't he just told Bobby to go? Having his father here was like having a college frat brother staying over. You had something in common, you knew you did, but you couldn't for the life of you see what it was.

"Why did you get married?" Leo asked during a lull in the game.

Bobby hit the mute button and swiveled to look at him like he'd grown another head. "Which time?"

"Any of them," Leo said shortly.

Bobby blew out a breath. "Seemed like the thing to do, I guess."

"Were you ever in love?"

Bobby's face split into a grin. "Every single time, my boy."

Leo felt a pang in his gut. "How is that possible?"

His father shrugged. "It just is. What's this about?"

Leo leaned his head back on the seat, closed his eyes. What did it matter? It would be in the papers before too much longer anyway. "I'm getting married," he said shortly.

"You don't sound happy about it."

"I don't know how to feel."

"Is she pregnant?"

"Yeah."

Bobby made a sucking sound with his teeth. "It's the right thing to do, then. You'll figure it out." Then he stood and put a hand on Leo's shoulder. "It'll work itself out, son."

"I'm sure it will," Leo said, oddly regretful that his father had nothing else to say. Bobby squeezed, almost as if he wanted to say something else, but then his hand fell away and Leo heard his footsteps retreating across the floor.

A few moments later the elevator doors whisked closed, and Leo knew that Bobby was gone. He took out his mobile phone and stared at the face for a long while before he brought up his contacts. He had to let Allegra know before she read about it in the papers. But he couldn't stand to talk to another person tonight, so instead he typed out a message.

Getting married. To Anna Constantinides. Just wanted you to know. Papers will have a field day.

He lay the phone down for barely a moment when it buzzed again.

Wow! I take it more happened on that island than you let on. Congratulations. I think. ☺ Oh, Leo. Please tell me you're happy.

Leo hesitated only a moment before he typed the answer he knew Allegra needed to hear, whether it was true or not.

Don't worry, A. I'm happy.

CHAPTER TEN

ANNA slept pretty well, considering all the stress of the day before. She awoke late, ordered breakfast in her room and dressed hurriedly in navy trousers and a cream blouse with tiny buttons that went almost to her throat. She left the last few unbuttoned so she could wear her pearls, and brushed her hair into a long, thick ponytail fastened loosely at the base of her neck. It was a departure from the usual updo, but it felt like the thing to do today.

She put the brush down and sighed at her reflection. She should be happy. Leo had said he would marry her. Their baby would be safe from scandal. And yet what he'd said to her last night still ate at her. Did she want to be married for the baby's sake or for her own?

She'd thought she was doing this for the baby, but a tiny part of her nagged that she wasn't. That Leo was right and it was herself she feared for. Was she truly that much of a coward?

She thought of the headlines the day after the photo of Alex kissing Allegra Jackson had first appeared in the paper. She'd been stunned by the report that he'd bought an engagement ring for this woman when it was she who had been wearing the official ring.

And then the reporters had started calling her every hour of the day and night, wanting a quote, wanting to catch her in an unguarded moment. Wanting to humiliate her even more than she already had been. She'd gone into seclusion on Amanti and prayed for the storm to pass. It hadn't, though the attention had lessened somewhat as the press focused more and more on Alex and Allegra's whirlwind romance.

Even her crash with Leo had only garnered a bit of attention, more for the spectacular circumstances of the crash and rescue than because she'd been alone with a notorious playboy. She'd been surprised by that, but she'd taken it for the rare gift it was.

But when she married Leo, when her secret was out, it would all change. She only hoped the storm would pass quickly, and she'd be free to live her life out from under the microscope of the media.

At precisely a quarter to eleven, Leo arrived as promised. Her heart turned over again at the sight of him. He wore a charcoal suit with a maroon shirt unbuttoned at the neck. It was stylish and daring and fit Leo to perfection. She envied him the ability to get away with color and still look so powerful and masculine. He made her seem dull in comparison, but perhaps it was the truth. She was dull.

And she wanted to keep it that way. She'd had enough color in the form of media attention to last her a lifetime. Shame flickered to life inside her.

Have you ever considered that perhaps you are more worried for yourself than you are for the child?

"I've made an appointment with one of the city's top obstetricians," Leo said to her. "We'll need to be going if we're to make it on time."

"Is that necessary?" she asked, gripping the door frame. "I feel perfectly fine. And I'd prefer to find someone on Amanti after we're married."

Leo frowned. "I'm not sure how you envision this wedding happening, Anna, but it won't happen today. And it won't happen on Amanti. We are marrying here. And we're staying here."

"I can't stay in London," she said automatically, her pulse throbbing. "I'm the Tourist Ambassador to Amanti. I have things to do. A home, family—"

"So go back to Amanti," Leo said tightly.

She squeezed her fingers on the door frame until her knuckles were white. "I can't do that."

"Then we have an appointment to keep, don't we?" He turned without waiting for an answer and strode down the hall toward the elevator. Fuming, she grabbed her purse and a light jacket and followed him. They took the elevator down to the ground floor and emerged in the bright sunshine of a clear London day. A minute later they were in his limousine, crawling through traffic like everyone else.

"I didn't come here to stay," she said coolly, though her pulse beat erratically beneath her skin.

Leo swung his head around to look at her. "You expect me to leave my business and move to Amanti because you wish it?"

"No. But surely we can work something out."

"What is it you suggest?" he asked.

Anna shrugged. "I could go back to Amanti after we're married. You could visit from time to time—"

"Out of the question," he said. "Did you not hear a thing I said to you last night?"

Her ears felt hot. "I heard you."

"Then you'll know that we're staying here. For the time being."

"Why?" she burst out. "You don't really want this marriage, or me, so why make it any harder than it needs to be?"

His gaze was so very cool. Unemotional. And yet she thought she saw a glimmer of heat behind those dark coffee eyes. "How do you know what I want, sweet Anna?"

She dropped her head, stared at the purse she clutched in her lap. "I don't want you to pretend, Leo. I know this isn't easy for you, and I appreciate that you're willing to help me—"

He made a noise that brought her head up. His expression, she noted, was patently furious. "You act as if this were an immaculate conception. I believe it takes two to make a baby."

"I know that," she said quietly.

"Then stop attributing motives to me that are designed to make you feel superior."

His words stung. "That's not it at all," she snapped. "But I have eyes, Leo, and I can sense when someone is unhappy. You'd rather be waking up this morning with the lovely Donna, not taking me to the doctor, so don't *you* pretend you're offended by anything I have to say. You'd rather this baby didn't exist, and you'd rather I was back on Amanti and nothing more than a memory."

He leaned toward her, his jaw set in a hard line. "If you're always this charming, it's no wonder Prince Alessandro found my sister more appealing."

Her skin prickled with heat as a sharp pain daggered into her. "Are you always this cruel?"

"That depends," he said. "Are you always this self-righteous?"

She stared at him for a long moment, locked

in battle—but she suddenly felt so defeated, as if life had conspired to knock her down at precisely the moment when she was already at her lowest. Anna put her face in her hands, breathed deeply.

"I'm trying to do the right thing," she said, her voice coming out muffled and weak. Which made her angry. She wasn't weak, dammit! She was strong, as strong as she needed to be to protect her child.

She dropped her hands, thrust her chin up. She would not cower before him.

"There's the dragon lady," he murmured. "If only you would bring her out to play when the press dares to mock you."

"It's an impossible battle to win," she said with a haughty sniff. "And I'd rather save my energy for other things."

The flame she'd seen in his gaze earlier flared to life again. "Yes, perhaps that's a good idea after all."

Anna felt herself coloring. *Cool. She must be cool.*

She might not be a queen-in-training any longer, but she hadn't spent years learning to be serene and unflappable for nothing. She held her head high, determined to be professional and businesslike. "How soon can we be married?"

Leo chuckled. "Eager, are we?"

Even the roots of her hair felt hot. Anna folded

her trembling hands over her purse. "I'm eager to move on with the plan," she said. "Before I start to show."

"It will take at least two weeks, possibly three."

She felt her jaw drop. "Three weeks?"

"I'll do what I can, but two weeks is the minimum time needed. You won't be showing by then."

"We could go to Amanti," she said practically. "The wait time is seven days."

Leo shook his head. "That's hardly worth the trip, Anna. Besides, I can't leave my business at the moment."

"You left your business to go to Santina for the engagement party," she said.

"Yes, and I lost several days, most especially when we crashed on the island. Being out of touch with my board of directors for two days during negotiations for a property in Brazil was a bit, shall we say, chaotic."

She didn't like the delay, but what else could she do? She already knew that once the baby was born, everyone would count backward. What did two—or three—weeks at this point matter?

She turned her head away from him. The limo had ground to a halt near Marble Arch, and happy tourists took photos and gawked at the white structure. They looked so carefree it made her ache. When had she ever been that carefree?

On the island, a voice whispered.

Except it wasn't *quite* true, was it? She'd definitely had cares—would they be rescued, what would the press say and so on—but she'd felt more like a different person there than she ever had before. A person without so many worries. A person who could swim naked with a gorgeous man and make uninhibited love on a secluded beach.

Anna clenched her fingers around her purse strap. She could still see him naked, his golden body so hard and perfect in the Mediterranean sun. Leo was flawlessly made, tall and lean and muscular in all the right places. He'd smiled on the island. Made her laugh. Made her moan and beg and shudder.

It had meant so much to her, she realized. Too much. While he'd returned to London and continued as he'd always done, she'd thought of him endlessly.

Despair flickered around the edges of her soul, but she refused to let it in. So she'd lost one man she'd been promised to and another she'd given herself to. So what? Others had it worse, didn't they?

And she had a baby on the way. There were new, more important worries to contend with.

In spite of the traffic, they arrived at the obstetrician's office located in a quiet Georgian town house on a side street a few minutes before the scheduled appointment. Leo exited the car first before reaching in for her, glancing up and down the street as he did so.

Anna's heart lodged in her throat as she sat on the edge of the seat with one leg poised over the pavement. "Do you see anyone?"

"No," he said curtly. "But it doesn't hurt to be on guard."

No, it certainly didn't. She didn't know how long it would take the press to discover her whereabouts, but she didn't imagine it would be long considering the way Leo's family always seemed to appear in the tabloids.

She joined him on the street, clutching his arm as she put her heel in a grate and nearly lost her balance. Leo held her hard against him, steadying her with an arm around her body as they came together breast to belly to hip.

It was the first time she'd been so close to him since the island, and she swallowed, her hands pressing against his chest for balance. They stood that way for a long moment, Leo gazing down at her as she stared back at him, her entire body humming with his nearness. His eyes dropped to her mouth.

Anna held her breath, surprised at how desperately she suddenly wanted him to kiss her. His fingers skated along her jaw, and her eyes drifted closed. His mouth claimed hers oh-so-lightly that she almost wondered if he'd meant it to happen.

Her heart beat like a trapped bird, her body straining toward his. She wanted the kiss to be hotter, harder, more intense—and yet it was perfect just like this. So achingly sweet and tender.

He lifted his head, and then set her away from him as he took her hand and led her into the doctor's office.

Eight weeks pregnant. It didn't seem possible, and yet the technician explained that the math had to do with the day of her last menstrual cycle and not the date of conception. Anna stared at the tiny bean on the screen as tears filled her eyes. She was really, truly expecting a baby. Leo's baby. She turned her head to look at him. He sat beside her, his gaze riveted to the screen. She reached for him without thought and his fingers closed around hers, squeezing softly.

For the briefest of moments, she thought it might be all right. That everything would turn out okay. Together, they would protect this child. Love this child. But then the technician turned on the Doppler and the sound of the baby's heart filled the room. It beat so fast that Anna thought there must be something wrong.

"The heartbeat is perfectly normal, Mrs. Jackson," the technician said in response to her cry.

"I'm not—" She stopped, swallowed. She felt so guilty, as if the technician would know that she wasn't actually Leo's wife yet.

Leo had filled out the paperwork and she hadn't bothered to check it. She'd answered the questions while he ticked off boxes. It reminded her, forcefully, that this was simply an arrangement. They would not be raising their child together, or at least not in the traditional sense. Leo didn't love her. A wave of depression washed over her at the knowledge.

"That is, thank you," she said smoothly. "I'm relieved to know it."

The remainder of the appointment was routine. The doctor asked questions, prescribed antinausea medication, told her when she would need to consider taking a birthing class and informed her when the next visit should be and what would happen then.

And then she was back in the car with Leo and they were pulling away from the curb, leaving Dr. Clemens's office behind. Anna chewed the inside of her lip. There was a pain in her chest, right beneath her breastbone, that wouldn't go away. Not a physical pain, but an emotional one.

What kind of mess had she gotten herself into? What had made her think she could barrel into Leo's life and ask him to marry her for the sake of the baby? What had made her think she could do it and remain untouched? Sitting in that room with him just now, his hand wrapped around hers while they listened to their baby's heart, had been one of the most significant moments of her life. How could she feel this way and not acknowledge that at least some of it was due to him?

"How are you feeling?" Leo asked.

How was she feeling? Lost, confused, alone. Uncertain. But she blinked away the moisture in her eyes and turned to him. "I'm fine."

He smiled for once, a rakish grin that had her heart turning over. Did he have to be charming when she was trying to keep her emotional distance? Why couldn't he keep snarling and frowning?

"It was a bit overwhelming," he admitted, and the breath squeezed in her lungs.

"Definitely." She smiled back, though the corners of it trembled. She hoped he didn't notice. "I have a feeling it's going to stay that way for quite some time yet."

He sighed, his expression troubled. "I think you're right."

She bit her lip, glanced away. It hurt to see him look like that. As if everything in his life had made perfect sense until she arrived in it. "I'm sorry, Leo."

He looked surprised. "For what?"

She took a deep breath, her heart burning. "For everything. If I'd been stronger on the island—"

"Stop," he said, his voice suddenly rough and edgy. "I was there, Anna. I know what happened as well as you do. And I was every bit as much involved in the decision process that got us to this point. Stop trying to insinuate it's solely your failure that created this situation."

"I didn't mean…" But she did, didn't she? She meant that he was simply a man, a rogue, acting on adrenaline and hormones and that she was the one who should have been smart enough and moral enough to put a stop to the sexual heat between them before it got out of hand. By inference, she was accusing him of thinking with his penis.

Of not thinking at all.

He was insulted, and rightfully so. Anna toyed with her pearls out of habit. Would she ever know the right things to say to this man? A lifetime of etiquette training, and she still couldn't manage to be diplomatic when it counted most. She was not the cool, serene woman she'd always thought she was. What a joke to think she could have been a queen when she could barely govern her emotions when it counted most.

"You're right," she told him. "I'm sorry for suggesting I was the only one who should have been in control."

"I know you think you're supposed to be in perfect control of yourself every minute of every day, but that's not the way it works, Anna. You're human. You're allowed to make mistakes."

She dropped her gaze. "I know that." And even if she didn't, she was learning that mistakes were not completely avoidable.

"I'm not quite sure you do. You live by your calendar and all that bloody training you did to be Alessandro's wife. You think that rigidly controlling every moment of every day will keep you from faltering."

"No one wants to be made a fool of," she said in defense. And yet it felt like such a weak defense now. She'd been made a fool of more in the past month than she ever had in her life, and she was still here. Still kicking.

"Of course not. But it's only when you care so much that anyone has the power to do that kind of harm."

"That's easy for you to say," she snapped, feeling pinned in from all sides. How could you *not* care when people said the most awful things about you? Printing lies to sell papers without a care for the truth? *She* knew what they said wasn't true, but not everyone did. And it hurt to see censure or pity in the eyes of those around her.

He had no idea what she'd been through, what she would go through if anyone found out she was pregnant before she was ready for them to do so. Santina and Amanti were far more conservative than the world Leo inhabited.

"When have you ever been the subject of negative attention? When has anyone ever said anything less than glowing about you?" she demanded.

He looked at her so steadily that she felt the need to drop her gaze from his. She wouldn't, however. She would hold steady and be brave, no matter what he was about to say. And she was suddenly certain, whatever it was, that she wasn't going to like it.

Once more, she'd blundered. She knew it in her bones.

"Before I was born, sweet Anna." His smile was smooth, polished. "My father had an affair with my mother while he was still married. He was at the height of his football career then, and quite the cad. When news of her pregnancy hit the papers, his first wife divorced him. He denied he was my father, of course. It was all the rage for weeks. You can look it up online if you're curious."

He sounded distant, detached, but she knew it had to bother him still. The way he spoke so carefully, his voice devoid of emotion. His expression sadly mocking. As if to say, *See, it's not so bad. I survived.*

"But you're a Jackson now," she pressed, because she didn't know what else to say. Her palms were damp, her skin prickling with heat. *Keep digging yourself a hole, Anna.*

"Yes. Another tabloid adventure when I was ten. My mother died in a drunk-driving accident, and I inherited not only her money, but also the DNA test she'd had done to prove paternity. After a stint in court, Bobby finally decided to do the right thing."

Her heart throbbed for the boy he'd been. He'd lost a parent who loved him and had then been forced onto another one who had tried to deny him. How terrible would that have been for him? "That must have been difficult," she managed.

He shrugged as if it were nothing. "It was a long time ago. I've moved beyond it now."

"But that doesn't change the hurt." How could it? How could you ever forget that someone hadn't wanted you? She'd grown up in a household where she was cherished, the beautiful, talented, bright daughter. And yet she hurt because she'd failed her parents, failed the King and Queen of Santina. Because Alex hadn't wanted her.

"You really are a sensitive creature, aren't you?" Leo asked. "You've lived your life in a bubble and you've been terrified to step outside it. But now you have, Anna, and you have a choice. Be brave, face it head-on, or crumple and let them defeat you. They *will* find out about the pregnancy. You can't keep a secret like this in our circles. Are you prepared for it?"

She sucked air into her lungs. Was she? Because she knew he was right. She'd come here knowing all the while it was a secret that wouldn't remain hidden for long. "That's why I'm here, Leo. I'm trying to prepare for it in the only way I know how."

"Then I hope, when the news breaks, you aren't hurt by it."

"If I am, I'll get over it. I've had a lot of practice recently." She said it to be brave, but inside she quaked.

He took her chin in his fingers, held her steady, their gazes locking. "You are a dragon lady, Anna. The fiercest, strongest, bravest woman I know. You survived a plane crash, two days on a deserted island and more bad press than any one person should have to endure. And you've done it all with grace and dignity. You will survive this, too."

His words pierced her to her soul. No one had ever, *ever* called her fierce or strong or brave. Competent, organized, pretty—yes. But fierce?

"It's my intention," she said softly.

"Excellent."

He tilted her chin up, and then leaned in and kissed her. The touch of his mouth was a pleasurable shock. His lips were hot against hers, his mouth infinitely more demanding than it had been on the street in front of Dr. Clemens's office. Anna melted into the kiss, though she told herself she should be more reserved with him. More careful. The only person who could get hurt in this situation was her.

Leo was nothing if not famous for his exploits with women. What meant the world to her was simply passing time to him.

But, like it or not, she felt something for him. She'd known it for the past month, though she'd denied it to herself over and over. Leo made her feel things that Alex never had. She felt beautiful, alive. Wanted, needed. Perhaps they were false sensations, but they were wonderful while they lasted. While she believed them.

His tongue slid across the seam of her lips and she opened to him, unable to stop the little moan that escaped her when their tongues met. He was the only man she'd ever kissed. And she didn't feel deprived by that fact. No other man could kiss her like this, she was certain. No other man could make her feel hot and achy and itchy and wonderful all at once.

Leo pulled her closer, the warmth of his body sinking into her flesh. He tilted her head back to give him better access, one hand cupping her jaw while the other slid to her waist. The touch of his fingers burned into her, through the fabric of her shirt and jacket.

He was her Kryptonite, weakening her until she couldn't resist.

"I've missed this," he said. "Missed you."

"Leo, I—"

He kissed her again, and she lost whatever she wanted to say. But her mind raced ahead, took her back to last night, when she'd first seen him walking out of the Leonidas Group headquarters building. He hadn't seemed to miss her at all then. He'd been so utterly self-assured when he'd strolled out of that building with a woman on his arm.

She pushed against his chest, lightly but firmly, and he leaned back, gazing at her through heavy-lidded eyes. Sensuality was as natural to him as breathing, she thought. She wanted to pull him back to her, forget her confused thoughts and lose herself in the promise those dark eyes made to her.

But she couldn't. "Last night, you were with Donna. If I hadn't come along…"

He blew out a frustrated breath. And then he looked down his fine nose at her. "You do realize that I am quite capable of going without sex for more than a day or so, right? Perhaps even weeks at a time. Being seen with a woman does not equate to having gone to bed with that woman."

She felt a stab of guilt. Once more, she was accusing him of thinking with his penis. A tiny, jealous—yes, jealous—corner of her insisted it must be true. He was Leo Jackson, lover of women, serial breaker of hearts.

"But you were planning on it."

"Probably," he said unapologetically. "But not for another week or two at least. Perhaps longer."

Anna sniffed, both chastened and irritated at once. "Then I'm sorry I ruined your plans."

Leo smiled, a sharp predatory smile that made a tingle start in her toes and work its way deep into her core.

"I'm not," he said. "I've a new plan I like much, much better."

CHAPTER ELEVEN

THE next few days were a whirlwind of appointments and appearances. Photographers had started to show up whenever Leo and Anna appeared in public together. He'd told her to expect it, but she still cringed every time. Inwardly, of course. Outwardly, she smiled and posed and tried to look ecstatically happy.

The headlines screamed at her each morning: *Jilted Bride of Santina's Crown Prince in Torrid Love Affair with Notorious Playboy; "I Had No Idea Anna Was in Love with Leo Jackson," Shocked Friend Says; Love Blooms Between Marooned Couple—But Were They Really Marooned, Or Was it Planned?; Crown Prince Alessandro Calls Anna—Come Back to Me, He Begs.* And the worst one of all: *How Long Will Lucky Leo Last This Time?*

Anna crumpled the morning tabloids and made a noise of disgust. He looked at her over the cup of coffee he'd poured from the silver service sitting nearby.

"It's ridiculous how they make these things up!"

"Surely you aren't surprised."

She ran a hand over the back of her neck, rubbed absently. "No, of course not. But it infuriates me anyway. You'd think they have nothing better to do."

"You did insist," he said. Yes, she had insisted on seeing the papers. When she'd sent the order to the front desk originally, Leo had come barreling in soon after, grumbling at her that it wasn't a good idea. She would get upset and that couldn't be good for the baby.

When she'd pointed out that she'd be more upset *not* knowing, he'd relented, albeit reluctantly.

Now, Leo got to his feet and came over to where she stood near the window, looking out over Hyde Park. The sun was shining today, and people strolled along the sidewalks and sat on park benches. Pigeons congregated around a man throwing something onto the ground. A red double-decker bus glided by on the street below, the top open and filled with tourists craning their necks and aiming their cameras.

Leo's hands settled on the back of her neck, and then he began to rub. Anna bit her lip to stop the moan that wanted to escape. It felt so good to have his hands on her. She wasn't quite sure if it was soothing in the way he intended it to be or titillating.

"You're tense," he murmured against her ear, and an electrical zap of energy shot down her spine, gathering in her core. Leo hadn't touched her since that kiss in the car, other than perfunctory touches for the cameras. She'd thought then that he'd wanted to make love to her again, that he intended to seduce her into his bed. It had excited her and frightened her at the same time.

But he'd done nothing since, and she'd been humming with frustration. It was better this way, she told herself. Better because this marriage would be temporary. Leo must have decided it, too, because he'd not pursued the issue when surely he must have known how easy it would be to send her over the edge. She was a mass of sensation waiting to happen. A collection of tinder anticipating the match.

"I keep expecting something worse," she said, her skin tingling wherever he touched. His fingers were sure as he kneaded her shoulders and neck.

"Something worse than Lucky Leo?" She could hear the smile in his voice, but she wasn't nearly as amused as he was.

Finally, something to focus on that would distract her from the sensation of his hands on her skin. "That is a rather disgusting name, considering how you earned it."

"By bedding six lingerie models simultaneously."

"It's not funny, Leo," she said, turning to look up at him.

His smile didn't fade. "Perhaps not. But what you desperately want to know, sweet Anna, is if it's true."

She dropped her gaze from his, a jealous fire flaring to life in her belly. *Jealous?* "You couldn't be more wrong," she said haughtily. "It's a vile exaggeration anyway."

His laugh was soft, deep, pulling at something elemental inside her. "Slightly. There were only four of them."

Anna stepped away from him, certain her cheeks were flaming scarlet by now. Leo with four women. Leo, naked and surrounded by *four* women. She didn't want to imagine it. A hot, sharp dagger of anger pierced through her heart. She wanted to choke someone. Four someones. "I said I didn't want to know."

"I'm only telling you the truth, Anna. Why keep secrets when we're about to be married?"

She wrapped her arms around herself. *Because this isn't real! Because it's a game to you!* The words swelled against the back of her throat, aching to escape, making it hard to breathe for the barest of moments. But she swallowed them back, refusing to let them out. "I don't see any need to confess deep dark secrets. This is an *arrangement,* not a true marriage."

He was still smiling, but she could see the hard glint in his eyes. As if she'd angered him. Or insulted him.

"Yes, of course. How could I have forgotten? You only need me to help you get through this difficulty, and then it's back to Amanti where you can play the proper lady. Though perhaps a slightly tarnished one, since you will have been married to me."

A throb of guilt beat a new tempo in her veins. "That's not fair," she said. "You twist my meaning."

The hard look was still there. "Do I? From the first, you've impressed upon me the importance of your reputation. Your status as the *ex*-bride-to-be of a future king." He tsked. "This must be so embarrassing for you, Anna. You've lain down with a mongrel and come home with fleas."

She flung away from him. He twisted everything she said, made her seem so awful and shallow when she was only trying to be fair to them both. To who they were as people. They didn't know each other well, it was true, but she knew what he was. What he'd always been. He'd never denied it, and now he was angry with her over it?

"You act so wounded! But tell me the truth, Leo—did you really want to be a husband and father? Is that what you see yourself doing? Because if so, why didn't you marry Jessica Monroe?"

He didn't react, and yet she knew the name had affected him. The air had changed between them when she'd uttered the name of the woman he'd been linked with in L.A. Grown heavier, thicker, tenser. She waited for him to speak, both fearing and needing to hear his answer.

When he did, his voice was cool. Detached. Clinical. "Jessica and I came to a mutual decision."

But Anna wasn't letting it go that easily. "And then she married some other man six months later and adopted a baby."

"We had different goals."

"Is that what it's called?" Bitterness churned in her belly. How could he not admit the truth when it was right there for everyone to see? He'd lived his life in front of the tabloids, sleeping with and casting off women with the kind of frequency with which most men changed their shirts. *Leo Jackson* and *family man* were not words ever used together in the same breath.

He'd practically said as much to her on the island.

"My relationship with Jessica Monroe has nothing to do with my relationship with you," he said tightly. She had the distinct impression that he was leashing some deep anger—or hurt?—within him. It gave her pause, but only for a moment. "*We* are getting married, and we have a child on the way."

"I've not forgotten it, I assure you," she said crisply, the blood beating in her temples, her throat. Something was going on between them that she didn't quite understand, and it infuriated her. Bothered her. How could she engage in conversation with him and still not quite know what either of them meant by the words they said? It was like going through a carnival fun house and not knowing what to expect around the next corner. "But I still don't believe it's your first choice of occupation."

He was going out of his mind with desire for her. Leo was still furious at their conversation of that morning, but he'd shaken it off as best he could and had taken her out to look at potential homes. He'd been putting the task on the back burner since he'd been so busy lately, but once Anna had arrived with her proposal of marriage, there was no getting past the fact it was high time to find a place and buy it.

Now, they were touring a two-level exclusive flat in a period building in Knightsbridge. Anna had grilled the estate agent on the amenities and led the way through the five-hundred-square-meter property. The agent had finally retired to the walkway out front to smoke a cigarette and make phone calls while he waited for them to finish.

Anna stood in the center of one of the upper bedrooms, staring at nothing that Leo could see. He took a moment to admire her form. She was, as always, buttoned up tight in a cream sweater set and gray skirt with, surprisingly, platform heels that made her legs so long and sexy. The pearls were a fixture around her neck, of course. She was playing with them, as she always did when she was upset or nervous or simply concentrating on something.

Her long dark hair was loose today, and he ached to thrust his fingers into the heavy mass as he took her body for his pleasure. Anna never wore her hair loose. The effect was about to kill him. He'd never been as achingly aroused as he had been for the past hour, watching her bare legs and round bottom as he followed her through the flat.

There was also, he had to admit, a simmering brew of despair and anger mixed in with the arousal. She was convinced he had nothing to offer in the way of being a husband or father. He wasn't sure he did either, but it was damned depressing to think of her leaving him once the baby was born. He'd been thinking about it all morning, and found himself surprisingly affected by it. He wanted to punch something. He wanted to rage and howl and expend a great deal of energy by doing *something* that required him to push himself to physical extremes.

Base-jumping. Mountain climbing. Extreme hiking across the Sahara.

Barring that, he wanted to lock Anna up and never let her out of his sight.

It was true that he didn't know the first thing about babies. They terrified him. So tiny and delicate and dependent on adults to take care of their needs. What if he was terrible at it? What if letting Anna go back to Amanti to raise their baby was the best choice for all of them?

And yet the thought of Anna and his child leaving him to his previous life of empty sex and meaningless relationships made him feel strangely forlorn. What if Anna met someone else and married him? That man would become his child's father, and Leo would have no business in their lives whatsoever.

Something deep and elemental inside him responded with a resounding, *No!*

"I'm not sure, Leo," Anna finally said, cutting into his thoughts as she turned to him in the empty room. Her voice echoed down from the high ceilings.

"Not sure of what?"

"It's gorgeous, but I'm not sure it's you. I see you in a penthouse somewhere, with sleek modern furnishings and a city view."

A flicker of annoyance slid across his soul. "It's not about me, Anna. It's about us. You will have to live here, too."

She dropped her gaze from his, and a current of anger and misery flared to life inside him, scorching him with the force of a thousand burning suns. And yet, could he blame her for thinking what she did? For thinking he was incapable of being what she wanted and needed him to be?

He'd made a second career out of being the kind of man women didn't say no to. He'd never met a woman he couldn't charm straight out of her knickers, and he'd never hidden that fact. Nor had he hidden the fact he wasn't the settling-down type. He'd never thought he would want to. The idea that he might after all gave him pause.

"Jessica wanted to get married. I didn't."

Anna's head snapped up, her jade-green eyes wide. He didn't know why he'd said it since it confirmed everything she thought about him, but he felt compelled to continue. He loved it when she looked at him, he realized. There was a little kick, right beneath his ribs, every time.

"She had a grown daughter, but she wanted a new baby. The roles in Hollywood were drying up for an actress her age. I believed she was latching on to the idea of marriage and a baby as a new challenge in life. She believed I was wrong. The split was mutual."

"Did you love her?" she asked, and he sensed that it cost her something to ask it.

Leo blew out a breath. The answer would do him no credit, but he wouldn't lie. "No."

She blinked. "No? Just like that, no?"

"If I'd loved her, would I have let her go? Or would I have done everything in my power to make her happy?"

"I see," she said.

He didn't think she saw anything. He and Jessica were similar in personality. Neither of them demanded anything from the other. They'd had a good time together. Love had never entered into the equation, for either one of them.

But then the arguments had begun. Small at first, escalating later as Jessica Monroe, once prized for her face and body, had started to weary of the fight for new roles. He'd never quite understood, as she remained to this day one of the sexiest women he'd ever known. But Hollywood was fickle, and that fickleness had driven Jessica to want more from him than he was willing to give.

Ironic that he now stood here with a woman

who was not only pregnant with his child, but that he'd also agreed to marry.

He closed the distance between them suddenly. She took a step back, but he caught her and pulled her to him. He didn't know why he had to hold her, but he did. He needed to feel her soft, warm body against his. Needed to know she was real, that their baby was real. He'd never quite known his place in life, never understood where he fit in in the Jackson family. He was the odd man out, the one who'd come in from the outside and tried to belong. Well, maybe Angel knew that feeling, too, but it was different—her father hadn't denied she was his and refused to have anything to do with her. She wasn't a Jackson by blood. He was, though he wasn't sure it had ever meant anything to him.

Anna put her hands on his chest as he caught her close, her head tilting back. She did not try to escape. In fact, he felt a tremor run through her. That faint vibration that let him know she was not unaffected. That she still wanted him as much as he wanted her.

Oh, she'd been good at pretending she did not—but only when he didn't touch her. When he touched her, he knew. And he wasn't prepared to show her any mercy. Not any longer.

"Do you ever think about it?" he asked. "Those two days on the island when there was nothing but sand and sea and *us?* You and me, naked beneath the hot sun?"

Her eyes were green pools of mystery. And warmth, he realized. Warmth for him. She usually hid it, but she wasn't doing a good job at the moment. It gave him hope, though for what he wasn't quite certain.

"I've thought of it," she admitted, her cheeks flushing as she spoke. Such lovely, lovely color, he mused. "How could I not?"

A low throb of arousal pulsed at the base of his spine. He wanted to take her here, now, in the middle of this room with the estate agent outside and the bright London sunshine streaming through the tall paned windows. "Then why are we merely thinking about it," he murmured, "when we could experience it again? In a bed this time, sweet Anna, with all the romance and tenderness you deserve."

"I—I'm not sure that's a good idea," she said, her gaze dropping to study her fingers where they rested on his shirt.

"How can it be a bad idea? You burn for me, Anna. You want me."

"That doesn't mean it's a good idea."

"Doesn't mean it's a bad idea, either," he told her, dipping his head to skim his lips along her jaw. She tilted her head back, her fingers clutching him. His body was stone. Hot, hard stone.

"Leo…"

"We're marrying, Anna," he said, trying not to make it sound like begging. Was he begging? An interesting thought, really. But he would, at this moment, do anything to get her naked and beneath him again. A singular thought. "Shouldn't we see if this could work between us before we assume it will not?"

Before she could answer, he heard a door open and shut, and he knew the estate agent had returned. Anna took advantage of his distraction to disengage from his embrace. But it wasn't a rejection. That much he knew. She tucked a strand of her hair behind her ear and folded her arms over her body. It wasn't a defensive gesture so much as a protective one.

Triumph surged in his bones. She would be his again. Soon.

Tonight.

CHAPTER TWELVE

A TRIO of boxes arrived within a couple of hours after she'd returned to the hotel. Anna directed the porter to place them on a table. Once she'd given him a tip and he'd gone, she turned her attention to the pretty white boxes tied in red ribbon. A card was on the top of the smallest one.

Wear these tonight. Eight o'clock for dinner.

She opened the smallest one first. A pair of slender designer heels with crystal studs on the straps made her heart kick with excitement. She'd never hidden the fact she loved beautiful shoes. Just because she wore conservative clothes didn't mean she needed to wear ugly shoes. That would be a sin against nature.

Next was a box with an electric-blue lacy thong and a matching strapless bra that made a tendril of heat uncoil in her belly. Leo wanted her to wear these tonight because he hoped to see her in them. She wasn't so dumb as to believe otherwise. Nor was she so certain of her answer that she wasn't going to put them on.

When he'd held her in the flat earlier, she'd wanted nothing more than to lie in a soft bed with him, naked skin against naked skin. She knew what awaited her when she did: heat and passion and physical pleasure so intense it would make her sob with joy. She wanted that again, even while it frightened her.

She wasn't afraid because she feared sex with Leo. She was afraid because she feared the truths she might have to admit to herself once he stripped her of her defenses. She turned to the last box with a little shiver of excitement dancing down her spine.

It contained a sequined dress in chili-pepper red. The dress was strapless, of course, and fitted through the bodice, hips and knees until it suddenly burst free in a gorgeous fantail. It was bold, far bolder than anything she'd ever worn in her life, with its blazing-hot color and sleek fit.

Her heart thrummed as she picked it up and went to stand in front of the mirror with it. Everyone would notice the woman who wore a dress like this. Could she bear the scrutiny right now?

Did it even matter? she asked herself a minute later. The press was already scrutinizing her. Since she'd started to appear in public with Leo, photographers had become a fixture in her life once more.

In the end, she decided to put the dress on. And the underwear. She left her hair long and loose, curling the ends so they fell in soft waves over her shoulder. A check of her reflection in the full-length cheval glass featured a woman she hardly recognized. A bright, sassy woman who walked into a room and owned it.

She'd never felt like she owned a room before. She'd been counting on her status after she'd married Alex to make her feel that way, but the truth was she should have learned the art long before. For herself alone.

A few minutes before eight, Leo arrived. He stood in the doorway with his hot coffee-colored gaze drifting over her and she felt as if an explosion had detonated inside her. He was resplendent in his custom-fit tuxedo. The white of his shirt contrasted sharply with his tanned skin and dark hair, making him seem even more devilish than he was. His sensual lips curved in a smile that whispered of sex and sin, and her heart went into a free fall.

She didn't even realize that she'd pressed her hand to her chest until he frowned.

"Are you feeling well?" he asked suddenly, coming into the room and taking her in his arms. "Is it the baby?"

"I'm fine," she managed. "I just felt light-headed for a moment."

And that was the truth. She'd taken one look at Leo and something inside her had shifted for the tiniest moment, taking her breath along with it.

"We can stay in," he said, looking concerned. "I'll order dinner up—"

"No, I'm fine. Really." She clutched his arm. "I want to go out. I didn't put this dress on for nothing."

He smiled, too, but there was worry in his eyes. "And a lovely dress it is, sweet Anna. You should always wear bold colors. They suit you."

She glanced down at the glaring red fabric. Count on Leo to see what she couldn't see for herself. When she'd looked in the mirror, she'd known he was right about the color. "This is a giant leap for me. I'm not accustomed to calling attention to myself."

"You should be," he said, his voice rough and soft all at once. Was that a kernel of need she heard? The idea thrilled her. "You are stunning, Anna. Marvelously stunning."

She laughed, but the sound was nervous, high. Could he tell? "Thank you for the dress. I would have never picked it."

But Leo had. Because he saw something in her that she was only just learning to see for herself.

It warmed her, made her pulse kick again. She was prepared for it this time.

"But do you like it?" he asked softly.

"I do, actually. I feel quite special in it."

Leo's smile had the power to make her heart flutter. "Because you are special, Anna." He took her hand and kissed it. "Never doubt it."

The restaurant he took her to was very exclusive. He was greeted by a fawning maître d' and staff, and then they were shown to a table in an empty dining room. The room was exquisite, with deep mahogany paneling on the walls, a frescoed ceiling and crystal chandeliers. The single table was set with crystal wine and water glasses, heavy silver flatware and a profusion of cream roses in a silver vase at the center.

After they were seated and the maître d' walked away, Anna glanced around the empty room and then back at Leo. He lifted an eyebrow, as if waiting for the question he knew must be coming. She laughed, then pressed her hand to her mouth and tried not to. Nerves, she told herself.

He reached over and took her wrist gently, removing her hand so her laugh sprang free again.

"Leo," she said. "This is crazy! Did you buy the restaurant?"

His smile was genuine. Pleased. "No. But I did buy the night."

She shook her head. It was unreal. Romantic. "We could have eaten with other people."

"Not tonight. I wanted you to myself."

"You've had me to yourself nearly every day."

"Not the same," he replied. "It never lasts long enough. Tonight, however, we'll have as much time as we want."

"There are staff," she pointed out, feeling bubbly inside nevertheless. "They aren't going anywhere, I assume."

"No, and later there will be an orchestra."

She blinked. "An orchestra?"

"We've never danced, Anna. I want to hold you in my arms on a dance floor."

She looked down at the white napkin carefully folded across a charger plate bordered in tiny gold scrollwork. Her heart felt as if it would burst from her chest any minute. She was happy, happier than she'd been since the island, and it worried her. What if it all fell apart tomorrow?

"You might be disappointed," she said softly.

"I doubt that." His voice was strong, sure, as if he'd never doubted anything less in his life.

"What if I step on your toes?" she asked, trying to lighten up the moment. Because, for her, it was too intense. Her skin felt too tight, stretched thin over the weight of emotions boiling inside her.

"Can't happen," he said. "You spent years training to be a queen. Queens don't step on toes. Or, if they do, it's quite deliberate."

She laughed again. "So if I step on you, you will chalk it up to malicious intent?"

"Most definitely."

A bow-tied waiter appeared just then with wine for Leo and a nonalcoholic cocktail for her. They talked about small things once he was gone—the weather, the state of tourism in Amanti as compared to London—and then the food began to appear.

Anna found that she was starving for once, and she ate everything placed in front of her, whether it was a seared *fois gras* on a bed of baby greens, a grilled filet with béarnaise sauce or a truffle-stuffed mushroom. Everything was delicious.

After the meal was cleared away and dessert served, Leo placed a velvet box on the table. Anna put her fork down, her pulse skipping into full throttle.

"What is it?" she asked, unable to make herself reach for the small black box.

"I think you know, Anna."

"It's not necessary," she said, though it hurt to say it. She wanted a ring to be inside—

But she wanted the reasons to be real. Anna's breath shortened. Could that really be true? Did she want this to be real?

She did. Oh, God, she did. She wanted him to

be marrying her because he wanted to, not because he had to.

Fickle, fickle Anna. This wasn't what she'd wanted when she'd come to London in the first place. Then, she'd only been thinking of her baby and protecting him or her from scandal. Protecting *them both* from scandal, if she were honest with herself. She'd wanted Leo's help, and she'd wanted to continue to play the martyr, the woman who needed no one or nothing to see her through life.

Now, she was realizing that she wanted so much more it frightened her.

"I think it is necessary." He pushed the box toward her.

She picked it up with trembling fingers and popped the top open. The ring was exquisite. A brilliant cut diamond of at least five carats in a platinum setting, surrounded by another two or three carats of smaller diamonds. The ring sparkled like fire in the candlelight, and she felt a pinprick of guilt and sadness. She'd pushed him into this, and she had no one to blame but herself if it wasn't real.

"Well?" he asked.

"It's beautiful," she said, her voice coming out far more hoarsely than she wanted it to.

Leo stood with a growl and took the ring from the box, which he tossed aside as if it were nothing. Then he put it on her finger and kissed her hand, his warm breath sending tiny fingers of sensation crawling down her spine. When he tilted her head back and kissed her, she didn't resist. She opened to him, her heart filling with love and despair in equal measure.

Love.

She'd been denying it to herself, but she couldn't do so any longer. Anna's heart throbbed with pain and fear and so much love she wondered how she'd denied it for so long. She loved this man, had probably loved him since the moment on the island when he'd kissed her on the forehead instead of the mouth because he'd realized her first kiss should be special. He'd been so tender with her, so thoughtful and selfless. He'd always put her feelings first, and he'd urged her to be her own person without regard to what others wanted from her.

He hadn't done those things because he loved her, she knew that, but it was what made him the kind of man she could love. The man she *did* love.

Oh, God.

His mouth moved over hers so expertly, so hotly, that she wanted nothing more than to melt into him and forget everything but the two of them. He'd planned a romantic evening, given her a ring, but she reminded herself that he was simply doing

what she had asked, playing a role she'd wanted
him to play in order to protect the baby.

And she had no one but herself to blame. She
was in love with this man, the father of her child,
but he did not feel the same, no matter how beautifully he kissed her.

He lifted his head, his eyes glittering with need,
and her heart squeezed with all she was feeling.
With all she could not say.

"Damn the orchestra," he murmured, pulling
her to her feet. "I'm through waiting."

Leo didn't take her back to his place. Not because
he didn't want her in his space, but because it
was Bobby's flat. And Bobby had taken plenty
of women there, both when he was married and
when he wasn't. Hell, Leo suspected he still did,
though not when Leo was in town.

To take Anna there would be wrong. Anna was
not a bit of fluff. She was the mother of his child.
His wife-to-be.

He took her back to the Crescent. The ride was
silent, fraught with tension as they sat on opposite sides of the limousine. Leo did it to keep from
tearing her dress off and taking her inside a car
gliding through the London streets at night. He
had no idea why she kept her distance. Perhaps
for the same reason.

They rode the lift standing at opposite ends

while the lift operator hummed and let passengers on and off. Leo wanted to kick everyone off and speed to the fifth floor, but instead he contented himself with watching Anna. She glanced up at him on occasion, her lovely face flushed. She licked her lips, and a spike of pain shot to his groin. He needed her so badly he was beginning to think he might embarrass himself once he was inside her.

When they arrived on the fifth floor, he swept her into his arms while she sighed and strode purposefully toward her door. He thought of fluffy puppies, of sunny fields of grass, of cows munching contentedly—anything but the woman in his arms. He was too completely aware of her. She was in his blood, his bones, and he wanted her utterly.

But he had to think of other things, or their night of bliss would become a minute or two of hurried coupling.

They reached the door and, with a swipe of the key card, were in.

The instant the door closed, her eager mouth fused to his. Leo groaned as he set her down and backed her against the door they'd just entered.

Her hands were on his tuxedo jacket, shoving it from his shoulders until he let it drop at his feet. Next she went for his belt. He found the zipper of her dress and slid it all the way down, pushing the garment down her lush breasts until he forced her to stop and step out of it before continuing with his trousers.

"Beautiful Anna," he said as he tossed the dress onto a chair. She stood there in the electric-blue underwear and heels he'd picked out for her, and she looked even more amazing than he'd dreamed she would. In spite of her protests, he turned her so he could view her lovely bottom in the thong panties. Her cheeks were bare, the thinnest slice of fabric disappearing between them before emerging again in a thin strap he wanted to tear apart with his teeth.

He dropped to his knees and worshipped that bare bottom with his mouth while she gasped. He'd never seen anything more beautiful than Anna's body. Her skin was golden, soft, and he wanted to touch it forever. Wanted to explore every inch of her while she moaned and sobbed and begged him to take her.

He needed her to beg him, he realized. He needed to know she wanted him as desperately as he wanted her.

"Leo," she gasped as his fingers slid beneath her panties and found the wet, hot center of her. He touched his mouth to the hollow of her back, slid his tongue up her spine and then nibbled her ear while his fingers found her most tender spot and stroked against the hot little ridge of flesh.

"Do you want me, Anna?"

She nodded, her eyes closed, her cheek pressed against the door.

"Tell me," he said.

"I want you. I want you so much."

He increased the pressure of his fingers as she began to moan. She shattered with a sharp cry, and then he was turning her, shoving those panties from her hips while she unsnapped his trousers and slid her hand beneath his underwear to wrap around his length.

She made a noise of approval. And then he was grasping her buttocks in his hands, lifting her against the door as his blood roared in his head. She wrapped her legs around him, knowing where he was going with this.

Another moment and he plunged into her as far as he could go. She took him greedily, her body so wet and ready it made him groan. The feelings washing over him were too much to process, so he shoved them down deep and concentrated on what he did best.

"Leo," she gasped as he slammed into her again and again. "Yes, yes, *yes*..."

He lost his mind. Lost what was left of it anyway. He drove into her as desperately and as precisely as he could manage. Had it ever felt this good? This right? Had he ever, ever wanted it to continue without end? Had he ever cared more for someone else's pleasure than his own? Of course he'd always made sure the women he bedded were happy, but had he *cared?*

When she flew apart, he knew. Her body gripped him hard, squeezed him as he thrust into her.

"Leo," she cried. "Leo!"

He gripped her harder, drove into her until he was spent, until he came in a hot rush that stole his breath. And then he swept her into his arms, took her to the plush queen bed in the adjoining room, and did it all over again.

Morning came too soon. Anna awoke slowly to the smell of coffee and hot food, her entire body feeling more languid and relaxed than it had in a very long time. She was boneless, a mass of satisfied nerve endings and raw emotions.

She turned over in the bed, encountered nothing but pillows and sheets. Leo had clearly gotten out of bed already. Her heart turned over at the thought of him last night, of all that glorious single-minded male lust focused upon her lucky, *lucky* body.

He'd taken her with such animalistic passion against the door, and again in the bed, giving her no quarter at all, no mercy, as he drove her relentlessly toward shattering climax after shattering climax. But early this morning, in the hour after dawn, he'd made love to her much more tenderly, spinning pleasure up slowly and thoroughly until it crested like a high tide.

She'd loved every moment of it, craved it yet again, though it had only been a few hours. But hadn't that been the way on the island, as well? Warmth flooded her as she remembered.

Simply put, Leo Jackson was a drug she didn't want to quit.

Her drug of choice walked in then, carrying two cups of steaming liquid. He was wearing absolutely nothing, and her pulse skipped wildly, a trapped butterfly in a jar.

"Surely you didn't answer the door like that," she said evenly.

He grinned. "Of course not, darling. There was a towel. I seem to have lost it. No doubt to impress you."

"Lucky me."

He bent and kissed her, then handed her a coffee. "Lucky you indeed," he said. "That's decaf, by the way. With cream and sugar, the way you like it."

She took a sip, her lashes dropping over her eyes. He knew how she liked her coffee. It made her heart clench tight in her chest, but she told herself not to read more into it than it was. It was simply coffee, the way she liked it, and decaf because caffeine was bad for the baby. Nothing more, nothing less. He'd had coffee with her enough over the past few days to know what she wanted.

It was not a declaration of love.

Love.

Her stomach did a slow flip. The feeling was still so new, so raw, and sometimes it snuck up on her and grabbed her by the throat. She wanted to tell him, wanted to spill the words and ease the pain of keeping them locked up tight, but she was scared, too. Scared he wouldn't return the feeling, scared that he would look at her pitifully and say something noncommittal.

She couldn't stand it if he did. Better to be silent and hope he felt the same way than to speak and find out he didn't.

She reached out and touched the tattoo on his abdomen, traced the iridescent scales gently. His muscles clenched in response. It was a beautiful piece of art, seemingly alive in the soft light, but it must have hurt like hell when he'd had it done.

"Careful, or you'll wake the sleeping dragon," he said huskily.

"Oh, I think I can handle a dragon," she replied, arching one eyebrow.

He grinned at her. "Indeed you can. Dragon lady."

"Why did you get this?"

He shrugged as he settled on the bed beside her

with his coffee. "A youthful decision, no doubt fueled by alcohol and bravado."

"You can't get a tattoo while drunk, Leo. No reputable studio will do it. And this is too fine not to have been done by a brilliant artist."

"No, I wasn't drunk, more's the pity since it hurt so damn much. But I believe I made a drunken wager that led to the tattoo."

"You could have said no," she pointed out.

"I made a bet, Anna. I could hardly renege."

Her heartbeat accelerated at the thought of him carrying on with something that he'd thought better of simply because he'd given his word. She didn't like to think of the implications to their situation now. Her pulse grew thick in her ears. "Do you always do what you promise, even if it turns out to be a bad idea?"

"I like to think I don't commit to things in the first place that are bad ideas. The tattoo is, as you say, beautiful. I don't regret it at all."

It was inevitable, however, that he must regret *some* things. Would she be one of them? She told herself to stop being fanciful, that tattoos weren't women, but she couldn't quite help it. She wore vulnerability like a second skin this morning. "But you do regret some of them in the end, I imagine."

He set the coffee down on the bedside table. "Who wouldn't? That's life, my darling."

She must have been frowning hard, because he leaned over and took her coffee cup away. Then he kissed her until she clung to him, lips and hands and body. Until desire flared to life inside her, hot little fingers of need caressing her and making her ache for him.

But instead of sliding her beneath him and making love to her again, he swung his long legs off the bed and stood. "Now come, you need to eat something. It's been a while since dinner."

Anna tried to push away the hurt throbbing through her at being rejected, though it wasn't *really* a rejection so much as a postponement. Still, it stung more than it ought when she was feeling so vulnerable.

She threw back the covers, determined to be strong, and reached for her robe. "You are the one who interrupted dessert," she reminded him.

"Did I? And here I thought I gave you a much more satisfying dessert."

Anna laughed as she tied the belt on her robe. "What arrogance," she teased lightly, though dread lay heavy on her heart. "Perhaps I would have preferred the cheesecake."

He stood there before her, one leg thrust indolently out to the side, his magnificent body still naked and rippling with muscle, and swept a hand from his shoulder to his groin as if to showcase the goods. "I am, you must admit, quite worth the interruption."

"I wouldn't dream of denying it," she said.

She left him getting dressed and walked over to the breakfast table. There were eggs, sausage, tomatoes and toast beneath the silver lids. Her folded newspapers lay on the table nearby, and she picked them up, wondering what silly thing the press had managed to say about her and Leo today. It was too much to hope they'd lost interest, of course. The Santina press had nothing else to do. The British tabloids were no better, though at least they filled their pages with plenty of celebrity gossip and WAG tales. Back home, she was front-page news. Here, it was a toss-up.

Not today, however, she discovered when she unfolded the first newssheet. The headline blared at her while her insides churned and a hot little flame began to lick at her.

She read it all the way through and then started again, until the moment Leo snatched the paper from her hand, swearing violently and long.

But it was too late. The words were already imprinted on her brain. How could they not be?

Lucky Leo's Luck Runs Out—The Jilted Bride Is Pregnant!

CHAPTER THIRTEEN

"I'M SORRY, Anna," Leo said, his voice throbbing with anger. "I had hoped we would have longer."

She was still trying to process it. "They took a picture. Of us kissing in front of Dr. Clemens's office. How did they know so soon? And why did they wait to use it?"

Leo swore again and raked a hand through his hair. He looked murderously, furiously angry. She, however, felt nothing.

Or, rather, she felt numb. That's what it was. She was perfectly numb.

It wasn't what she'd expected to feel. It wasn't what she'd felt when the pictures of Alex and Allegra had appeared, along with the headline proclaiming her a jilted bride. That had been embarrassing, no doubt. This, however…this was a violation. Of her life, of her baby's life.

Of Leo's life.

He came and gripped her shoulders, thrust his face into hers and forced her to look up at him.

"It doesn't matter, Anna. We're getting married in five days. We're just going to have to deal with this sooner rather than later."

All her plans were wrecked. She'd wanted to marry so that by the time she began to show, the question of scandal would be dubious at best. Oh, sure, when the baby was born, anyone could count backward and figure it out. But it would be months past, and she would be a married woman with a new baby.

It had been perfect. And now it lay in ruins around her like a pile of bricks that only a moment before the wrecking ball hit was a house.

"How did they figure it out so soon?" she repeated.

Leo's lips thinned. "I don't know, but I intend to find out."

She held up her hand, the ring sparkling and dazzling in the bright morning light. Last night, she'd felt so special and hopeful when he'd taken her to dinner in an empty restaurant and given her this ring. It was everything a romantic night out should be, except for the fact it was staged. Staged because the marriage was already planned.

But she hadn't cared, really, once he'd kissed her and brought her back here. He'd smashed every notion she'd had about how this marriage would go. He'd stripped her barriers, stripped her body, and forced his way into her soul. He was a part of her, in more ways than one, and she loved him. She'd actually had *hope* after last night that everything would turn out well. That she'd be happy, and that Leo would be happy with her.

Until she'd read the paper and realized their secret was out. No one would ever believe there was anything between them but an adherence to duty for the child's sake.

Did she care? Did it matter?

It shouldn't matter, but she found that it did. How could they ever be happy together if their marriage began under a dark cloud of suspicion and scandal? How could she ever be sure that Leo didn't resent her for the circumstance of their marriage?

As the next few days passed, the scandal grew. The usual made-up nonsense got twisted in with the truth, and everything got blown out of proportion. She refused to talk to reporters, as did Leo— so they made things up. They found witnesses, paid doormen and waitresses and coat-check girls, to say anything and everything outrageous and untrue.

Leo grew stony and distant. They had not spent the night together since the evening before the story broke. And, much to her dismay, pictures of their lovely evening together appeared in the papers. Taken with a telephoto lens through a window, someone had caught the moment when Leo had kissed her senseless before taking her back to the hotel.

Now, it was all about appearances, about making everyone think they were blissfully happy together when they were anything but. Leo still took her to dinner, to the theater, to corporate events he had to attend. Photographers lined up in droves outside the venues, the flashbulbs snapping and questions popping like automatic gunfire.

Anna said nothing. Leo ushered her through the gauntlet with either a firm hand on her back or gripping her hand in his. He made no comment, though he did once stop abruptly when a reporter asked him what it felt like to be trapped into marriage by a gold-digging foreigner.

Anna had wrapped her arm around his and urged him to keep walking. After a minute in which she'd felt the tension stringing through him like a bow drawn to the breaking point, he'd done as she asked and continued down the walkway.

Her parents called. They were shocked, outraged and so disappointed. And yet, when her mother had begun to berate her for her impulsive nature, her father had hissed out a curse. A moment later, there had been a heavy silence.

"Anna," her father had said into the phone while her mother started to cry in the background. "You are our daughter and we love you. If this man is not what you want, come home. We will take care of you."

She'd squeezed the phone in her hand. "I'm getting married, Papa. It's what I want."

"Ne," he had said solemnly. "Then we are happy."

She'd hung up then, feeling miserable because she'd put them through so much. And even more miserable that her marriage to Leo was now overshadowed by her pregnancy.

Or, to be fair, it had always been overshadowed by her pregnancy. But at least it had been between the two of them and not the whole world.

The evening before the civil ceremony was finally to take place, Leo had a business dinner in a penthouse suite overlooking the Thames. Anna accompanied him at his request, since there would be spouses and partners present.

As they entered the penthouse, all the chatter died and a dozen faces turned to them. The silence was awkward until a man suddenly came forward and shook Leo's hand, welcoming him to the gathering. The ice was broken and people behaved normally again, mingling in small groups and chatting, eventually coming together for a dinner that had Anna seated across the table and several spaces down from Leo.

She felt uncomfortable, isolated, and her eyes strayed to Leo. He laughed easily, talked to the people seated on either side of him. Anna made small talk with the old gentleman on her right. On her left, a woman pointedly ignored her, only engaging in polite small talk when it was absolutely necessary.

Anna felt the stares all night. It wasn't that these people were scandalized. She was pretty sure they weren't, being as wealthy and connected as they were. Some of them had no doubt been victims of the press in the past, as well.

No, it was the way they looked between her and Leo, no doubt wondering if theirs was a marriage that would last. By now, everyone knew they'd been marooned on an island together. And everyone knew, clearly, they'd had sex.

Anna was pregnant, and Leo was stepping up to do the right thing. But, poor man, did he really want to be married to such an uptight woman as she? She was trying so hard, but she was still the woman she'd always been. She still liked her calendars and reminders and intricate plans. She felt grounded that way, and she wouldn't apologize for it.

But she'd allowed herself to wear color recently, and she'd even gone so far as to show a little bit of skin on her shoulders and arms. Leo had made her feel beautiful, and she'd felt confident enough to grow bolder in her choices. Tonight she'd chosen a pale pink sheath dress with tiny straps and a bolero jacket.

But she still wore her pearls and she still held her spine stiff and straight.

What a joke it had been to think she would have ever made a good queen. She didn't know how to relax, in spite of all her training. She was stiff, formal and uncomfortable when she believed people were scrutinizing her. As they would have done constantly had she married Alex.

She hid a yawn behind her hand and glanced at her watch. A quarter to eleven. Leo disengaged from the conversation he was having and came to her side as if he sensed her discomfort.

"Are you tired?"

"Yes. I want to go back to the hotel and go to bed," she said. *With you,* she silently added.

Leo made their excuses to the host and hostess, and then they were sitting in silence in the big limousine. Anna yawned again. She wanted him to hold his arm out, wanted to snuggle into the circle of his embrace and lay her head against his shoulder.

She wanted the warmth and happiness they'd had for that one night together. But it wasn't going to happen. Leo, it seemed, regretted their night. Whereas she thought of it as one of the best of her life. They'd almost been happy together. For the barest of moments, she'd thought they would make this marriage work.

That he would love her as she loved him.

Instead, he sat stony and cold and she was unable to break the silence between them. Unable to utter the correct words to make everything go back to the way it was when he'd taken her to dinner four nights ago and given her an engagement ring.

"It was a nice party," she said into the silence.

"Did you think so? I thought you were unhappy."

She colored in the dark, though he could not see it. "I wasn't unhappy."

He turned his head, and she could see the flash of his teeth. "You were. You hardly said anything tonight."

"That's not true," she replied. "I talked to those around me. The woman on my left at dinner was quite difficult, actually."

"Probably because we dated once, long ago."

Anna blinked. A sliver of anger uncoiled within her. And hurt. "Well, I should have guessed. Lucky Leo strikes again."

"Anna, I'm sorry."

"For what?" she said, trying to keep her voice light and gay when she felt anything but. Hurt and anger spun together in a vortex inside her, sucking her down with it. "You can't help that you've probably bedded half of London. Half of the *planet,* I should say."

"I'm sorry I didn't warn you when I saw her tonight. I wasn't pleased you were seated beside her, but whenever I looked in your direction, you seemed to be doing fine."

"My training, no doubt. I am a born diplomat." Hardly, but she wasn't admitting that particular failure to him tonight.

"It won't happen again, I assure you."

"How can you do that, Casanova? Are we to flee every dinner engagement where you've slept with someone present? I fear we'll never go anywhere."

He took her hand. She jumped at his touch. Her body began to melt, to need. Hot sparks flared to life in her belly, between her legs. It had been days since he'd touched her more than perfunctorily.

"You're nervous and upset. I understand. But let's just get through tomorrow, shall we? We have plenty of time to figure it out from there."

Get through tomorrow, get through tomorrow...

"Of course," she said, removing her hand from his lest she melt into a puddle of need and beg him to take her to bed and hold her close all night long.

He wanted to *get through tomorrow.* As if it were an ordeal to be endured. A sentence to be served. A penalty.

It hurt.

They reached the red awning of the Crescent and he helped her from the car. She deliberately took a step back when they were on the red carpet leading into the hotel. The flash of a bulb lit up the night, followed by another and another. Leo hurried her into the marble-and-glass lobby dotted with potted palms nearly two stories tall.

Anna disengaged from his embrace once they were out of sight of the photographers.

"Let's say good-night here," she said, needing to put space between them. Needing to think and plan and not *feel* so damn much whenever he was near. She could do this if she could only gain perspective.

He frowned. She thought he would say no, and then he tipped his head. "Very well. I'll pick you up tomorrow morning at ten."

She waved a hand in the air as if it were a trifle. "There's no need, Leo. The registry bureau is in the opposite direction from your office. I'll meet you there at ten-thirty. It'll preserve the mystery, yes?"

His brows drew down. "The mystery?"

"If this were a church wedding, you wouldn't be allowed to see me in the dress before I walked down the aisle. Let's attempt to follow the form."

His frown didn't dissipate. But he acquiesced. "If that's what you wish. I'll send a car for you."

"Very well," she said.

And then she stepped up to him and pulled his head down to hers. She kissed him with all the pent-up passion she possessed, triumphing in the groan emanating from his throat. His tongue slid into her mouth, tangled with hers, and she almost believed it. Almost believed he needed her as much as she needed him.

But he didn't. Or at least not in the same way. She disengaged from the kiss, straightening her jacket, and bid him good-night.

He watched her get into the lift. The doors slid closed and she turned into the corner, pressing her fist to her mouth and willing herself not to cry.

It was all wrong. Once more, it was all wrong.

She wasn't coming. Leo stood in the hallway outside the registry office where they were to be married and processed the information he'd just been given. Anna had not shown up, according to the driver he'd sent over for her. A call to her mobile netted him nothing. Another call to the front desk, and he learned that she'd checked out more than two hours ago.

Rage was the first emotion that coursed through him, scouring his insides like sulfuric acid, eating away at him until he wanted to explode into action. But what sort of action? Punching something would do no good, no matter how exhilarating it might feel.

Despair was the second emotion to pummel him. Somehow, that was harder to deal with. She'd left him. Anna Constantinides, his beautiful uptight Greek with her pearls and her veneer of cool competence that he knew hid a passionate, fiery nature. Anna was molten, no matter how hard she tried not to be. All the buttoned-up clothing in the world couldn't hide that sizzling beauty of hers, no matter what she believed.

He stood in that hallway with people passing around him, going on with their lives and jobs, and he felt suddenly bereft. Empty. As if she'd taken the light with her when she'd gone. He didn't understand it. Why had she left? Why, when this marriage had been so important to her in the first place?

He'd always known she was doing it for reasons that had nothing to do with him. The knowledge that she could dismiss him so easily in her calculations had pricked his pride, but had he given her any reason to do otherwise? His greatest fear was being a horrible father. His second greatest was disappointing Anna.

Twice, she'd pushed him from her life. The first time, he'd been angry and disappointed. This time, he felt as if someone had punched him in the gut. Repeatedly.

He knew what he had to do, the only course of action that made sense.

He had to go after her. He had to stop her before she left. It was the only thing that would halt the agony inside him.

And say what to her, Leo?

His mind cast around for the right words. He had to tell her that he *could* be a better person, that he *wanted* to be a father and a husband, and that he wanted her to give him that chance. That with her by his side, he knew he could do anything. He wasn't doomed to be his own father, wasn't doomed to a life of poor choices and empty relationships if he didn't choose to be.

Leo shot down the hallway, down two flights of stairs, and burst into the gloom of a rainy day. He didn't have time to wait for his driver to come around, so he hailed a cab. The trip to Heathrow took forever but he was finally there, finally bursting through the doors and sprinting for the British Airways counter to buy a ticket to Amanti. It was the only way to get through security to see her.

He strode straight to the VIP line and breezed through to the counter agent.

"I'm sorry, sir," the agent said when he told the man what he wanted. "But that flight is already on the taxiway."

"Then stop it."

"I'm afraid we can't do that, sir."

Leo wanted to haul the agent over the counter

by his collar and demand he stop the plane, but he knew that was the surest way to spend a few days cooling off in a jail cell. Instead, he slammed a fist against the counter and went back out into the rain, hands thrust in his pockets, stomach churning with rage and pain. Eventually, he hailed a cab and had it take him back to Knightsbridge.

She'd left him. She'd bloody well left him standing at the metaphorical altar and run away at the last damn minute. Because she knew he didn't belong in her life. His relationships with women had always been about the physical, never the emotional. He was damaged when it came to knowing how to share the parts of him that went deeper than the surface.

But he'd tried. With her, he'd tried. And it hadn't been good enough, had it? She'd seen through to the damaged parts of his soul and said, *No way*.

Leo didn't even bother drying off when he entered his father's apartment. He poured a glass of Scotch and slumped on the couch, raindrops sliding down his face and plopping onto his damp clothing.

Bobby found him that way hours later, still sitting, still staring at nothing. His clothes had dried, but they were now stiff and uncomfortable. He didn't care.

"What happened to you, boy?" his father demanded, coming over and taking the empty glass away.

Leo looked up, blinked. His eyes felt gritty, tired. "Got what I deserved," he said. "About time, too."

"What the hell are you talking about?"

"Anna. She left me."

Bobby thrust his lower lip out. "Mmm, I see." He perched on the edge of the table closest to Leo. "You love her?"

He'd been thinking about that for hours now. "Yeah, I think I do."

"Think? Or know?"

Leo rubbed a hand over his eyes, his forehead. "How do you ever know?" He knew he was asking the wrong man, not only because Bobby seemed to have an open-door policy on who he loved and how often, but also because Bobby had never yet offered him any advice of substance. But the lonely little boy inside him still wanted it to happen. Wanted his father to step up and be a father for once, not just another partner in crime.

Bobby blew out a breath and rubbed his hands on his knees. "You know because when she's gone it hurts deep down—" he put a fist to his torso, right below his rib cage "—right here. It hurts and it won't go away. No amount of alcohol can kill it. No amount of sex with other women can kill it. Nothing but time, if she won't take you back. And even then, it continues to burn."

Leo blinked. "Who did you feel that way about?" He was too surprised by what Bobby had just said not to ask the question.

Bobby leaned back, hands still on his legs. "Ah, well that's my secret to bear, isn't it? Suffice it to say I screwed up. But you can fix this, Leo. Go after her, tell her how you feel."

As if it were that easy. He'd tried that. It hadn't worked. Anna had left him without a word. She'd never given him the chance, and he was angry about it. Angry that he'd stood there in the airport and felt as if his world was crumbling from beneath his feet and there was nothing he could do about it.

"What if she doesn't care?"

That was the moment when Bobby said the most profound thing Leo would ever hear him say, even if they both lived another hundred years. "If she didn't care, I doubt she'd have left. Women don't run when they aren't scared of something. If all she wanted was your money or your name, she'd have said those vows faster than lightning. Trust me."

Bobby got up then and clamped a hand on Leo's shoulder. "I love you, Leo. I know I haven't always done right by you, but I love you. You'll be a terrific father, not because you had a great example to follow—and we both know you didn't—but because it's who you are inside. There's nothing you do that you don't excel at."

Leo felt tears pricking at the corners of his eyes. "Why haven't you said this before?"

It was...extraordinary. And just strange enough that he almost thought he must be dreaming.

Bobby shrugged. "Because I wasn't sure you'd welcome it. You're so damned independent—get that from your mother—and so competent that I feel a bit out of sorts with you."

"Out of sorts?"

"Hard to admit your kids know more than you do. If I opened my mouth and removed all doubt, would you ever respect me?" Bobby shook his head. "No, just seemed easier to spend time with you and hope you knew how proud you make me. I can't change the past, but I can let you know I'm here now. I've made mistakes, Leo, but I do love you."

Shame jabbed at Leo's conscience then. "When the story broke in the papers, I wondered for a moment if it was you who'd told them. Not on purpose, but inadvertently."

He knew better now, but his father had been the first flash of a thought. The guilt of it, however briefly it had entered his mind, ate at him, especially after what Bobby had just said.

His father shrugged again. "Of course you did.

Who else would be most likely to get drunk and open his mouth?" Then he patted Leo. "I've gotten better about that. It wasn't me, but I don't blame you for thinking it could be."

Bobby started toward the elevator and Leo stood to watch him go. "Dad," he said when the doors opened and his father stepped inside.

Bobby turned, his finger on the button. There was so much Leo wanted to say, so much he wanted to know. This relationship was a work in progress and might always be. But it had just taken a step forward that he'd never expected and there was only one response needed.

"Thanks."

The other man smiled, and then the doors closed and he was gone.

CHAPTER FOURTEEN

"IT SEEMS as if I was wrong about you," a voice said from behind her. "You aren't a dragon lady at all."

Anna whirled, her toes catching in the sand, and nearly fell to her knees. Fortunately, she did not. The early-morning sun was behind him, silhouetting his body in a nimbus of light as he moved down the deserted beach toward her.

But was he a figment of her desperate imagination, or was he real?

"Leo?"

"Expecting someone else?" he said as he came to a stop a few short feet away.

Anna shook her head because no words would come out. It *was* him. And she could hardly believe he was here. She'd left London nearly a week ago, and she'd regretted it every moment since. As he'd implied, she'd been a coward. Hot emotion welled in her chest, her throat, aching to spill forth. But she swallowed it down and stood there, watching him as he watched her. Neither of them said a word for long moments.

And then he broke the silence.

"You left without saying goodbye." There was a hard edge to his voice that made her swallow the lump in her throat.

"I know. I'm sorry."

"That's all?"

"What else do you wish me to say?" she asked, her heart throbbing with hurt and love and passion for this man. He was here and she wanted to throw herself into his arms, sob and beg him to give her another chance.

"Why don't you explain why you thought it necessary to run away without at least telling me you no longer wanted to marry me."

Her heart ached so much. "I wanted to tell you," she said. "I started to tell you."

But every time she'd tried to initiate the phone call, dread had gripped her by the throat and refused to let go. She'd finally realized that the only way to release him from his promise was just to go.

"You should have."

She shook her head. "I couldn't. You would have insisted on going through with it anyway, and I didn't want to do that to you."

Leo growled. And then he shoved a hand through his hair and turned to look out at the whitecaps foaming on the surface of the sea as they broke toward shore. "*You* wanted the marriage, Anna. *You* asked me."

"And you always keep your promises, even when you know you'll regret it later!" she cried, suddenly unable to hold it in any longer. He turned toward her and she ducked her head, embarrassed. "I couldn't bear the thought that you would regret me."

He looked stunned. "That's what this is about? The fact I made a bet over a tattoo and went through with it?"

It sounded stupid when he put it that way. Embarrassment flooded her. "Of course it's not about the tattoo. It's about you being the sort of person who honors his promises."

"My God, Anna, you frustrate the hell out of me. You wanted the marriage to protect the baby. What happened to change your mind? A bloody tattoo story?"

"Of course not," she said, stung. "I realized once the story broke that you were right. I did want the marriage for me, to protect *me*." She dropped her gaze to the sand, studied the tiny whorls made by sand crabs in the night. "I'm ashamed of that."

She heard him move, and then he was gripping her shoulders and forcing her to look up at him. She felt like whimpering at his touch, but she bit the inside of her lip and kept quiet. She knew she was pitiful.

"Don't say that, Anna. You thought you were doing it for the baby. You *were* doing it for the baby. No one should have to endure the kind of stories you've had to over the past few months. You had every right to think of how our child would have been affected."

A tear trickled down her cheek and she dashed it away. "But I had no right to force changes into your life because of my problems with the press."

His grip tightened. "Anna, this baby is *ours*. I want to be there for him."

"Or her," she added automatically.

"Or her." He pulled her into his embrace suddenly, and she closed her eyes and breathed him in. His heart was thrumming hard and steady, and his skin was so hot beneath his clothes. Searing her. Making her want. She curled her fingers into his shirt and just held him. For a few moments, she could allow herself to enjoy this.

"When I told you about the stories surrounding my mother's affair with my father, and the subsequent stories when she died—I was wrong when I said they didn't affect me. Of course they did. I've been living with their impact all of my life. It's made me who I am, Anna."

She tilted her head back to look at him. "Oh, Leo, I'm sorry."

"I'm not," he said. "I like who I am. But I like who I am with you even better."

Her heart skipped a beat. "You're only trying to make me feel better for wanting to force you into marriage."

He sighed. "Don't you realize by now, sweet Anna, there's no forcing me to do anything I don't want to do? I agreed because I wanted this marriage. I still do."

Her knees were suddenly so weak that if he wasn't holding her tight, she'd have sunk to the ground. "I thought I was forcing you into something you didn't want to do. And I walked out without an explanation. How could you still want to marry me?"

"Isn't it obvious?" he said, teeth flashing white in his handsome face. His eyes were so hot and intense as they raked over her face, daring her to believe.

"I—I'm not sure it is."

He shook his head, but his smile never wavered. "I love you, Anna. I love our baby. I like who I am with you, and I want to spend the rest of my life with you. I want to see you grow big with our child, and I want to be there when he—or she— comes into this world. I want to bring you coffee every morning, and I want to make love to you as often as possible. I want to unbutton your high-necked shirts and make you wear colors more frequently. I want you in my life, and I want to marry you so you can't ever run away again."

The tears she'd been holding in sprang free, sliding hotly down her cheeks. She told herself to hold it together, but it was far easier said than done. She put her forehead against his shirt and sobbed while he held her tight.

When she finally managed to compose herself, she lifted her head to find him gazing at her tenderly. "I thought you didn't care," she said, her breath hitching. "I thought you must hate me for making you go through with a marriage you didn't want."

He looked stunned. "What on earth made you think that?"

"You grew so distant after the story broke. All I wanted was for you to hold me, but you wouldn't touch me." She sniffled. "You wouldn't spend the night with me again."

He squeezed her tighter to him. "I thought you were too upset, that you weren't resting. I knew if I were there, you definitely wouldn't rest. Because I couldn't keep my hands off you."

"You seem to have done a good enough job of it." Her voice sounded small, hurt. She dropped her gaze to his chest, to where she was still clutching him tight.

He swore softly. "I couldn't touch you, Anna. Not without wanting to make love to you. It was safer to keep my distance. I wanted you to rest. It was only four nights. We'd have been together on the fifth."

"But I didn't rest," she said, her fingers trembling as she smoothed the fabric of his shirt. "I tossed and turned because I thought everything was ruined between us. I loved you so desperately, and I thought you despised me."

"Look at me," he said, and she raised her gaze to his. His smile made her heart turn over in her chest. Soft, hopeful, full of tenderness. "You love me?"

She blinked, stunned at the question. "I thought it was obvious."

His laugh was broken. "You forget how good you are at the serene thing." He slid his fingers along her cheek, into her hair. And then he breathed a great sigh. "I'm a lucky, lucky man. And I plan to spend a great deal of time taking advantage of my good luck."

He dipped his head, his mouth claiming hers in a scorching kiss that could have melted ten-gauge steel. Warmth blossomed inside her, rolling through her like hot syrup. She was melting with need, with love.

"I need you, Anna. Come home with me. Marry me. Today."

It was everything she'd ever wanted, ever

dreamed. Leo and her…and their baby. *Perfection. Bliss. Rightness.*

"Yes," she said. "Definitely, yes."

He groaned and squeezed her tight, as if he would never let go.

"Remind me," he said a few minutes later, between hot kisses to her lips, her throat, her cheeks, "to send Donna a thank-you note."

"Why is that?" she asked when he let her breathe again.

He lifted his head, his dark eyes glittering with heat. "She's the one who set the reporters on us."

A flash of anger rushed through her, but it was gone like a wisp of smoke on the breeze. How could she possibly be angry when she was so happy? "And that's a good thing because…?"

He grinned at her, and warmth filled her. "Because it opened our eyes to the truth."

And that, she realized, as Leo swept her into his arms and carried her back up the beach, was a very fortunate thing. Sex was fabulous. But love was better.

Fabulous sex *and* love? Bliss.

* * * * *

Behind the Scandal:

**An exclusive interview with
LYNN RAYE HARRIS!**

AN EXCLUSIVE INTERVIEW WITH LYNN RAYE HARRIS

Who is more scandalous—the Jacksons or the Santinas?

Oh, I think they are equally scandalous! The Jacksons are in-your-face scandalous, while the Santinas try to hide their dirty laundry behind closed doors.

Mirror, mirror, on the wall, who is the sexiest hero of them all?

I'm partial to Leo, of course! He is such an irrepressible flirt, and so sexy.

What secret would make the most shocking tabloid headlines about Leo and Anna?

I think maybe you'll have to read the book to find out! They have one or two...

Where does Leo take Anna for their one year anniversary?

To their own private island!

We just can't wait to hear about your writing process, can you talk us through your daily routine?

It's not very glamorous, truthfully. I wake up early, get a cup of coffee or tea, and go upstairs to my office. I usually check e-mail and see what my friends have been up to for about an hour, and then I open up the latest book I'm working on and get lost in the pages. Some days, the writing goes fabulously and I get a lot done. Other days, I stare out the window a lot. I might even shop for shoes (but don't tell my husband!). I also get interrupted by the two cats in my life who think I have nothing better to do than cater to their needs.

What do you think makes a good hero and heroine?

They need to be real. They need to feel like the kind of people you could know. Even though the stories take place in larger-than-life settings, often with very wealthy and privileged people, the characters need to have real emotions and fears. They have to be identifiable to the reader.

Did you have a favourite character in this novel?

Oh, I just loved Anna! She was so fierce and lonely at the same time. And of course Leo was the perfectly delicious hero she needed to sweep her off her feet. Watching him lose his cool over her was such fun.

What is it that you love most about writing your stories?

I love exploring how two people who should be all wrong for each other are meant to be together. I love writing about love. About emotions that are larger than life, and people who feel deeply and passionately. It just doesn't get any better than that!

What projects are you working on at the moment?

I'm always working on the next story about a handsome, sexy, dynamic man and the lucky heroine who gets to tame him.

We know it's tricky, but what is your favourite book of all time?

Oooh. How can I choose? I can't, so I'm

going to have to choose a writer instead. Shakespeare. He wrote the most amazing things, and explored human emotions so thoroughly. And I can quote random lines from the plays and sonnets, which comes in quite handy during trivia games.

Don't miss the last book in

THE SANTINA CROWN

Playing the Royal Game

by

Carol Marinelli

Available in August 2012 from Mills & Boon®

Turn the page for an exclusive extract!

'ALLEGRA!' She woke to the ringing of the phone and there was no time to gather her thoughts before answering. 'Allegra, it's me, Angel, what on earth's going on?'

'Hold on a moment,' Allegra said. 'Someone else is trying to get through.' She looked at the caller display, saw it was her brother Leo at the same time as she saw the ring on her finger and heard the bell that meant someone was at her door.

Oh, God!

'Angel…' She couldn't explain it to her step-sister right now—yes, they were close and they spoke about so many things, but this was more the sort of situation Angel might find herself in, not the other way around. 'I've got someone at the door. I'll have to call you back.'

Even as she put down the phone it was ringing again, her father this time.

She didn't answer it.

And she tried to ignore her doorbell, just

wanted a moment to gather her thoughts. A coffee would be extremely welcome, except whoever it was must be leaning on the bell, because it was ringing incessantly now. Kids meeting up at the underground for school often pressed it for the sake of pressing it, so she hit the display button to see the camera shot…and saw the face of Alex, pale and unshaven. He looked less than happy.

Well, he could have his ring back, Allegra decided—it had been a stupid game that had got out of hand.

'It's open.' She pulled on a dressing gown and turned on the kettle, then went to the front door as she heard him rounding the top of the stairs.

Somehow he looked both beautiful and terrible at the same time—his olive skin seemed tinged grey, his eyes were bloodshot and he was still in yesterday's suit.

'Coffee!' She could hardly stand to look at him she was so embarrassed—so she turned and headed to her small kitchen. 'Before we say anything, I need coffee…and by the looks of things so do you.' Her blasted phone was ringing and unable to face it she turned it off and then spooned instant granules into mugs. 'You can have the ring back.'

'Oh, no, you don't.' There was something in his voice that sounded like a warning, almost as if he were angry, and she turned around. 'You can't just get out of this.' He held up a newspaper. 'I'm as-suming you haven't read the papers or turned on the news.' Allegra went cold as she saw the photo. It was of her and Alex—him tenderly holding her hand and examining the ring that now seemed to burn her on her finger.

'At least—' she tried to stay calm, to think of a positive '—at least it wasn't a few moments later,' she said, 'when we kissed.'

'My kissing a woman would hardly be news-worthy,' Alex said, 'but that the Crown Prince of Santina has bought a woman a ring…'

'It was a mistake,' Allegra said. 'We'll say—' her mind raced for possibilities '—that we're friends, that I was simply showing you—'

'I have just spoken with Anna.' Alex chose not to go into detail; the conversation had been supremely difficult and one he did not want to examine just yet, let alone share. When Allegra asked after the other woman, Alex shook his head. 'Somehow I don't think she'd appreciate your con-cern.'

His words were like a slap, the implications of the one reckless day of her life starting to unravel.

'I have also spoken to my parents.'

'They've heard?'

'They were the ones that alerted me!' Alex said. 'We have aides who monitor the press and the news constantly.' Did she not understand he had been up all night dealing with this? 'I am waiting for the palace to ring—to see how we will respond.' She couldn't think, her head was spinning in so many directions and Alex's presence wasn't exactly calming—not just his tension, not just the impossible situation, but the sight of him in her kitchen, the memory of his kiss. That alone would have kept her thoughts occupied for days on end, but to have to deal with all this too, and now the doorbell was ringing and he followed her as she went to hit the display button.

'It's my dad.' She was actually a bit relieved to see him. 'He'll know what to do, how to handle—'

'I thought you hated scandal,' Alex interrupted. 'We'll just say—'

'I don't think you understand.' Again he interrupted her and there was no trace of the man she had met yesterday; instead she faced not the man but the might of Crown Prince Alessandro Santina. 'There is no question that you don't go through with this.'

'You can't force me.' She gave a nervous laugh. 'We both know that yesterday was a mistake.' She could hear the doorbell ringing. She went to press the intercom but his hand halted her, caught her by the wrist. She shot him the same look she had yesterday, the one that should warn him away, except this morning it did not work.

'You agreed to this, Allegra, the money is sitting in your account.' He looked down at the paper. 'Of course, we could tell the truth…' He gave a dismissive shrug. 'I'm sure they have photos of later.'

'It was just a kiss….'

'An expensive kiss,' Alex said. 'I wonder what the papers would make of it if they found out I bought your services yesterday.'

'You wouldn't.' She could see it now, could see the horrific headlines—she, Allegra, in the spotlight, but for shameful reasons.

'Oh, Allegra,' he said softly but without endearment. 'Absolutely I would. It's far too late to change your mind.'

The World of Mills & Boon®

There's a Mills & Boon® series that's perfect for you. We publish ten series and with new titles every month, you never have to wait long for your favourite to come along.

Blaze®
Scorching hot, sexy reads

By Request
Relive the romance with the best of the best

Cherish™
Romance to melt the heart every time

Desire™
Passionate and dramatic love stories